THE QUICK AND THE DREAD

A COLLECTION OF HORROR STORIES

ISBN-13: 978-1977688538
ISBN-10: 1977688535

Copyright © John Moralee 2014, 2015
Revised 2022.

The moral right of John Moralee to be identified as the author of this work has been asserted in accordance with the Copyright, Design and Patents Act, 1988. All rights reserved. No part of this publication may be reproduced or transmitted in any form or by any means, electronic or mechanical, including photocopy, recording, or any information storage and retrieval system, without the permission of the author. Any person who does any unauthorised act in relation to this publication may be liable to criminal prosecution and civil claims for damages.

This book is a work of fiction. All names, characters, businesses, organisations, places and events are either the product of the author's imagination or are used fictitiously. Any resemblance to actual persons, living or dead, events or locations is entirely coincidental.

The Skeleton was first published in Tricks, Treats and Zombies © AZT Publications 2016.
The Ripper Legacy was first published in The Mammoth Book of Jack the Ripper Stories © Robinson 2015.

Cold, Wet Hands was first published in Footsteps in the Dark © Flame Tree Publishing 2020.

Please visit www.**mybookspage.wordpress.com** to find out more about the author.

CONTENTS

Writing Horror 101 - 4
Cold, Wet Hands - 7
The Black Room - 23
The Skeleton - 39
The Man in the Mirror - 53
Do Fear The Reaper - 55
The Deadline - 57
Moonlight - 58
The Crack - 61
One Winter Morning - 62
Call of the Shakologoth - 63
Night Hunt - 73
Shell House - 75
666 Downing Street - 79
The Journal - 80
Thuds - 82
Eve - 102
Interview with a Zombie - 104
The Flash - 107
Sky and The Spirit Child - 119
Little Monster - 139
When the Bough Breaks - 149
The Ripper Legacy - 166
Writing Horror 102 – 189
Afterword - 192

WRITING HORROR 101

Someone broke into my house when I was at my computer struggling to start the first draft of a horror story. He sneaked up behind me with a knife, pressing it to my throat. The cold steel got my attention really fast.

"Don't move," he said. "Or I'll kill you."

Believe me, I had no plans to move with a knife touching my throat. The intruder had my full attention. I could see him reflected on the screen of my laptop, standing behind my chair. He was wearing a black mask with his mad eyes glaring at the fifty-eight words I'd written. I remembered to stay still as I spoke calmly, trying to act unafraid. "What do you want?"

"Shut up. I'm *reading*." His mouth moved as he silently read the few sentences on the screen. His sour breath tickled my neck.

I'd spent two hours writing only a few sentences because I was suffering writer's block. I'd deleted my first line and rewritten it a dozen times before coming up with a passable beginning. I was not happy with the result – but I hoped this crazy stranger was not an insane critic. Rule One of writing is NEVER SHOW ANYONE YOUR FIRST DRAFT. Especially madmen with knives at your throat. It took him over a minute to finish reading, which seemed like a long time for so few words. I waited. Scared and nervous. Two questions spun around in my head. Would he like what I'd written? Would he cut my throat if he didn't?

"No, no, I don't like this," he said. "You'll have to do better. It's garbage."

"That's harsh criticism. It's the first draft. I'm just working my way into the story, getting a feel for the characters and situation."

"No excuses. It's not good enough. Listen to me, Mr So-Called Writer. I'm your worst nightmare. I am your inner voice, buddy, the part of you that knows when you're writing your best and when you're coasting. I'm sick of waiting for you to feel inspired. Writers don't wait for inspiration. They write. They get on with their job. I'm here to give you some help writing something worth reading because you lack motivation. So, here's the deal. I'm gonna give you one great reason for writing hard and fast. You have one hour to write a horror story. It can be about anything as long as it is completed. If I don't like what you do, I'll cut your throat and leave you to die here in your grimy little study, where your body won't be found for a week."

He touched the cold blade to my neck, drawing blood, just to prove he was serious. I winced. His other hand showed me a stopwatch. Click. The timer started counting upwards from zero. The numbers moved worrying fast.

"Hey! I'm not ready!"

"Tough! You'd better get started," he said. "You have sixty minutes."

"Sixty minutes to write a story? I'll never do it. It takes me sixty minutes to get in the mood. I need thinking time."

"Fifty-nine minutes now. Stop procrastinating."

"Hey – I don't do that. I have a girlfriend."

"Ha, ha. Enough with the wisecracks. Fifty-eight minutes and thirty seconds. Write me a horror story. Now, Mr So-Called

Writer."

The masked man was a psycho, but he had the timer and the knife. I opened a new document in Word and stared at the white screen, seeing the black cursor blinking away rapidly.

The masked man was waiting.

I didn't want him to kill me – but what could I do?

I had no ideas ready.

I had no inspiration.

I could think of nothing.

The knife was hurting my neck.

Okay. Think! What was I going to do? Lull him into relaxing his grip on the knife? No. He was too alert – too wired. I would have to try writing a story, even though my mind was blank.

I leant forward and stared at the keyboard, settling my hands over the keys.

Less than sixty minutes to write a story?

I could do it. I could write a story in that time.

I wasn't going to let writer's block kill me.

I started typing for my life.

COLD, WET HANDS

The summerhouse was so far away. Maddy could barely see it on the horizon, where the silver-blue lake met the dark-green hills. She felt as though she had been swimming for days because her limbs were aching and the water's coldness had sapped her strength. As she increased the speed of her crawl, Maddy stared at the distant shore and wished she had never started her morning with a swim. She was no longer a fit teenager like she had been the last time she stayed at the summerhouse.

Ten years of adulthood – working in a law firm in Chicago, where her life consisted of sitting at a desk writing reports – had reduced her fitness and stamina to a dangerous level. After only swimming to the middle – an easy feat when she was sixteen – Maddy was too breathless to continue to the far shore. She had decided to turn back. But it was the same frightening distance to the summerhouse. For the first time in her life, Maddy was afraid of drowning. Her faster strokes didn't seem to shorten the distance. They were tiring her at her quicker rate. Ahead was a vast ocean and below her was a deep, dark hell.

Heart pounding, lungs burning, Maddy stopped swimming as a sharp pain in her side brought tears to her eyes. Not a stitch

– not now! Chilling water poured into her mouth, making her cough and splutter. It tasted brackish. She started choking. The pain of her stitch and the shock of the water in her lungs made her panic. Forgetting how to swim, she started to thrash and lose control, drawing more water into her lungs.

Before she understood what was happening, her head was under the water and she was sinking to the murky lake bottom, a trail of air bubbles coming out of her mouth and nose.

The surface was a long, long way above, but she could do nothing to slow her spiralling descent. Her peripheral vision was shrinking as oxygen failed to reach her brain – darkness creeping up on her from all sides.

As the last air bubbles left her mouth, Maddy knew she was dying. Her conscious mind was shutting down. She stopped struggling, stopped fighting. She closed her eyes.

Death was coming.

She could feel its warm embrace.

Maddy was at least twenty-feet down when her survival instinct returned. Her rational mind told her to do something, anything, if she wanted to live. By then she was in semi-darkness, not sure which way was up.

Something slimy touched her bare legs, feeling like oily hands trying to grab her and pull her down. Down! Yes! Her sense of direction was working again. *Got to go up. Got to escape. Swim UP!* Maddy kicked out and thrashed her legs, aiming herself upwards, until she burst out of the water into the hot sunlight, gasping for air.

She retched violently. After sucking in several long breaths, she trod water until her heart slowed and the chest pain subsided.

Terrified by her near-drowning, Maddy switched to a slow and steady breaststroke, keeping the summerhouse as her focus, her way home. When she finally reached the rocky shore, she climbed out, shivering and sobbing, relieved to be alive.

She staggered to a safe distance before flopping down on the grassy embankment, taking in deep, painful breaths. She wept like a little girl. After a couple of minutes, she had the energy to sit up and look back at the tranquil lake, feeling as though she had been betrayed by a lover.

Lake Kachika looked beautiful with the sunlight flashing on the water like glittering diamonds, but she would never trust the water again.

Maddy grabbed the towel left on a rock and wrapped it around her wet torso, hurrying onto the wooden deck leading to the summerhouse, where she saw her nineteen-year-old sister lounging in the sun, wearing a skimpy red bikini and heart-shaped sunglasses. Izzy was reading Proust's *Remembrance of Things Past* in the original French. She was also smoking a cigarette – a bad habit she'd started in college.

"You look like crap," Izzy said.

"Thanks. I almost drowned."

"Ah – that'd explain the pale vampire look. I thought you were auditioning for a new Twilight movie."

"Not funny. I was really scared. I thought I was going to die."

"Seriously?"

Maddy nodded. Tears stung her eyes.

Izzy looked concerned, abandoning her book and cigarette. "Hey – I'm sorry. I thought you were exaggerating.

What happened?"

"It's so stupid. I went under and nearly drowned because I forgot I'm not as fit as I used to be. It's a long swim when you're out of practice, believe me. I'm *never* going in that water again."

"Are you all right now?"

Maddy wanted to say yes, but nothing came out of her mouth except a miserable whimper.

Seeing her distress, Izzy jumped up and hugged her. "You're freezing. You might be in shock. Come on – take a nice hot shower. I'll make you a warm coffee."

"S-screw coffee," Maddy sniffled. "Give me that cigarette."

An hour later, Maddy was in her bathroom, vomiting into the toilet bowl, her head pounding with every pulse of her heart. She'd never felt as sick in her life. She moaned, heaving and heaving, a cold sweat coating her body. Eventually, her nausea subsided, but only after her throat was sore and her head ached like her worst-ever hangover.

She flushed away the vomit, then brushed her teeth, then showered. To fight the headache, she opened the medicine cabinet and found some long-expired paracetamol pills. Swallowing four pills with cold water, she looked at herself in the bathroom mirror. Her left eye was bloodshot, probably as a result of her close call with the Grim Reaper. It looked horrific, like someone had punched her. To hide it, she tried brushing her dark-brown hair over that side of her face, but it made her look like the creepy girl in *The Ring*. There was a pair of sunglasses on her dresser – so she went to get them. The bright sun through the windows gave her a stabbing pain behind her eyes. As soon as she slipped the sunglasses on, she felt instant relief, though her head still pounded. Feeling sorry for herself, she sat on her bed and checked her phone for messages. Nothing interesting on Facebook, Twitter or Instagram.

Sighing, she lay down and closed her eyes. She wanted to sleep. But she remembered the feeling of drowning and felt her heart racing. Sleep was impossible.

Maddy listened to the silence. The summerhouse used to be filled with sounds of talking and laughter, but it was quiet. During the summers when she was a kid, the summerhouse had always been full of friends and relatives visiting from all across the country, invited to stay by her wealthy parents. It sounded deathly quiet without them. Their parents had divorced seven years ago. Maddy remembered the good times they'd had as a family at the summerhouse before everything went wrong – before her dad left them for his PA and her mom married a Russian oligarch called Ivan. Deep down, Maddy wanted her parents to be there – happy together – instead of living on different continents.

Half-dozing, Maddy heard her sister's feet on the hardwood floor as she came into her room without knocking. Izzy's footsteps sounded wet as she lightly padded across the floor. Maddy heard Izzy stop next to the bed, breathing slowly. Izzy didn't speak – so Maddy assumed it was because her sister wasn't sure if she was awake or not. Maddy opened her eyes, ready to say something about respecting her privacy. Nobody was there – but she had *heard* Izzy in her room just moments earlier. There were wet footprints on the hardwood floor, leading from the closed door to the bed. Maddy frowned.

"Izzy, where are you?"

There was no reply.

"IZZY, WHERE ARE YOU?"

"Outside!" her sister called.

"Outside?" Maddy rushed to her window and looked down at her sister sunbathing on the deck. "Izzy, have you just been up here?"

"What? No. Why?"

"Have you been in my room when I was dozing?"

"No! Why?"

"I thought -" She sighed. "Sorry. Never mind. I must've been dreaming." But that didn't make sense because she'd seen the wet footprints. She was sure her own feet had been dry when she came up to her room. Maddy turned around and stared at the floor where she'd seen the trail.

The wet footprints had gone.

"What are you looking for?" Izzy said, wandering into the kitchen, where Maddy was staring into the refrigerator with no memory of having walked downstairs. Maddy had been standing there long enough to feel the chill on her bare legs. Since there were only bottles of water and expired orange juice on the shelves, she didn't know why she had been staring. She closed the door and faced her sister. "We need to go shopping. I'm starving."

"Good idea. Hey – what's up with your legs?"

Frowning, Maddy looked down at herself, noticing a nasty red rash on both of her lower legs, roughly in the shape of five long fingers. It looked like she had been slapped hard and the redness had not faded. "Urgh. That's weird. I must be allergic to whatever weeds are at the bottom of the lake. I remember it felt like slimy hands."

"They look like bruises. Your eye's burst, too. I didn't notice that before. Maybe you need to see a doctor, sis. You look terrible."

"No. I'm okay. I'll be fine once I put on some hydrocortisone cream."

There wasn't any in the summerhouse – so they decided to take their dad's Jeep into the local town to buy supplies for their vacation. They drove to Drury – a little coastal town a few miles north, near the border of Maine. Maddy bought everything she needed in the small mall, plus a whole load of candy and chips that was an impulse buy, then she joined her sister in The Blue Lobster, the best and only seafood restaurant.

Maddy loved the rustic charm. The restaurant's owner had given the interior a nautical theme – fishing nets, plastic crabs and starfish hung on the walls among photographs of sailing boats and brave fishermen in raging storms. The owner normally greeted them like old friends as they went in, but she was not there that day. Instead, a James Franco lookalike working as a waiter shamelessly flirted with her sister. He offered them the best booth by the windows, looking out on the harbour. Izzy flirted back, while Maddy wondered why the ridiculously handsome waiter had not even looked at her. Not long ago, she had been the centre of male attention on her visits to Drury. She hoped it was her bloodshot eye making her repulsive and not her general appearance. Being in her younger sister's shadow made her feel old and ugly. After the waiter had gone to help some other customers, Maddy sighed.

"That guy certainly likes you," she said. "But I think he

thought I was Swamp Thing."

"Here, wear my shades," Izzy said, passing her sunglasses across the table. "I can't stand looking at that funky eye. Dude, check out the size of the menus. They're huge. It's just like I remember when Mom and Dad used to bring us here. Hmm. I don't know what to pick."

"I'm having the surf-'n'-turf."

Izzy raised an eyebrow. "You're having *meat*?"

Maddy was puzzled. "Yeah, so?"

"You're *vegan*."

"I am? Oh. Yeah. I forgot." She'd been a vegan since she was sixteen. A Greenpeace documentary on slaughterhouses had convinced her that eating meat was wrong. But, for a strange moment, she had really craved a juicy steak.

"You forgot? Dude, you're acting weird. Seriously, you need to see a doctor."

"I'm fine. I just need to eat something." She spoke to James Franco's lookalike. "For starters, I'll have the chilli fries and the vegetarian pizza with a Coca-Cola. Regular – not diet, please."

"And what can I get you?" he said to her sister.

"What do you recommend?"

"The Special is good."

"I'll have that," Izzy said, looking at his name tag. "Thanks, Evan."

"My pleasure," Evan said. "What's your name?"

"Izzy."

"Cool name. I'll bring your meal in ten minutes. Have a good day, Izzy."

As he walked away, Izzy licked her lips. "He's hot."

"Yeah," Maddy admitted. "I wouldn't mind a slice of that myself. Yum-yum!"

They started laughing loudly. Five locals at a table turned and stared. Maddy found their hostile looks intimidating. What was their problem? Didn't they like laughing? They were wearing dirty blue uniforms marked with the logo of Greystone Fisheries. Most of the men were in their fifties or sixties. One had short salt-and-pepper hair and a long beard. His hairy arms were covered with tattoos of bare-breasted women entwined with snakes.

Maddy didn't like the way he looked at her.

I know him!

She felt a sudden, intense pain in the middle of her forehead, as though someone had jabbed her with a hot needle. The pain stunned her. She screamed something that made no sense.

"Gremlin!" she yelled, then she felt a hot liquid running down her face, into her eyes, stinging, blinding her.

Somewhere nearby, Maddy heard her sister calling her name over and over, but Maddy could not see her.

Everything was dark.

And cold.

And wet.

She was drowning again.

Maddy woke in a hospital bed, confused but pain-free. Her sister was there, along with a doctor with a friendly smile. He said some kind and reassuring words, then left them alone.

"What happened to me? How'd I get here?"

"You passed out in The Blue Lobster and I couldn't wake you up. Evan – the waiter – called for an ambulance. You were conscious when it arrived, but you were talking nonsense."

"Like what?"

"Oh, all kinds of crazy stuff. You called me Angela and insisted your name was Maureen."

"Maureen?" She didn't know anyone with that name. Or Angela. "That's weird."

"Yeah. It was creepy. The paramedics brought you here, where the doctors did a bunch of tests. They found nothing wrong with you physically, except for the rash and a mild fever. They gave you some antibiotics and fluids. The doctors told me you'd recover if you have plenty of rest." Izzy grabbed her hand and squeezed it. "Don't scare me like that!"

"I'll try not to," she said. "I don't remember any of that. Maureen and Angela? Why would I say those names?"

Izzy shrugged. "Who knows? The good news is you're going to be fine. The better news is Evan gave me his phone number. He's not just a waiter, you know. His mother owns the restaurant, so he was helping her out because they're short on staff. He's studying music in Portland. He's in a local band called Picklehead. They're doing a gig at the Rusty Nail on Friday night and he's invited me."

"I'm glad my illness got you a date. Can I get out of here now?"

"No. They want to keep you under observation until the morning, but I'll stay and keep you company. I'll find the clicker so we can watch some TV."

"I'm not in the mood for TV. You don't need to stay all

night. You need to get a proper night's sleep, too. Can you do me a favour before you go?"

"Anything."

"I need you to ask your boyfriend if he knows who the guy was at the restaurant with the sexist tattoos of naked women."

"That's a strange request."

"Yeah, but will you do it?"

"Uh – sure. I'll text him." She pulled out her phone. "I don't see the point of this, but whatever. Uh. Evan says he knows the guy. He's a regular. His name is Tad Peters."

"Tad Peters?" The name meant nothing, but it sounded familiar. "Izzy, any idea why I said the word 'gremlin' earlier?"

"No idea."

That night Maddy had a strange dream. She imagined herself naked and wandering around the moonlit town like she was lost, her long hair dripping with icy water. She was looking for something, but she didn't know where to go.

She stopped at a dark house with a small garden, where she slipped inside through an unlocked door without making a sound. Her bare feet left wet marks on the carpet.

She found Tad Peters snoring on a couch, passed out from drinking too much beer.

Without waking him, she leant over him and locked her mouth onto his as though kissing him passionately, though there was no passion in the act. Her tongue forced his mouth open.

Suddenly, brackish water was pouring from her mouth into Tad's throat, making him choke in his sleep. Tad opened his eyes and struggled, but she held him down with incredible, unnatural strength.

More and more water filled Tad's throat — until Maddy jerked awake in her hospital bed, vividly recalling the dream, her entire body soaked in a cold sweat.

The next morning, Maddy was feeling stronger when Izzy picked her up in the Jeep. The hospital food had been terrible, so they stopped at The Blue Lobster for breakfast. Evan served them.
"Have you seen Tad Peters today?"

"No – but his friends were here. One told me they saw an ambulance at his house last night. He's been taken to hospital with pneumonia."

"Is he okay?"

"I don't know."

I did that, Maddy thought. *I tried to kill him.*

"Something wrong?" her sister said.

"Yes. I had a dream about drowning him. Something's happening. It's like I'm not *me* any longer."

"What do you mean?"

"Tad Peters did something very bad. I'm sure of it, but I don't remember *what*. I need to see him. He has to tell me what happened. I'm going back to the hospital."

"Maddy, you can't."

"I have to see him!"

"Okay, okay. I'll come with you. Just don't do anything crazy."

Maddy and Izzy returned to the hospital. It wasn't hard to find out which room Tad Peters was in. Drury General didn't have the tight security of a city hospital. It was easy to enter his room with nobody noticing. Tad Peters was connected to beeping monitoring equipment. He was awake, but his eyes were unfocused. He stiffened when he saw Maddy.

"No!" he said. "Please don't kill me, Maureen. I didn't mean to hurt you. It was a mistake. I'm sorry. I'm sorry."

"How do you know me?" Maddy asked, but he didn't answer. His heart rate and blood pressure rocketed, triggering alarms. It looked like he was having a heart attack.

Izzy grabbed Maddy's hand, dragging her out of the room. "Let's get out of here, Maddy. We can't be caught in here."

Maddy hurried into the corridor before the doctors and nurses arrived. Luckily, the staff were too busy to notice Maddy and Izzy making a hasty exit.

"What the hell is going on, Maddy?"

"I don't know. Why did he think I was somebody called Maureen?"

"She must be someone he knows," Izzy said. "We can Google her."

"We can't Google a first name. There are millions of Maureens. We need a surname."

"If Maureen is a local person, she'll probably be in an old yearbook. I'll ask Evan for help."

Evan visited that afternoon, bringing a stack of yearbooks. "Why do you need these?"

"Just research," Izzy told him.

'Maureen' was a dated name – so they started looking in the yearbooks from the 1960s and 1970s. They found several. Only one was interesting. A girl called Maureen Nielsen. She had been a chunky girl with lank brown hair and bad acne. There was a deep sadness in her eyes like she'd never had a day of happiness in her life. She had been in the same class as Tad Peters. A

Google search revealed she had gone missing in 1972, aged fifteen.

"Izzy, this will sound mad, but I think she drowned in the lake. That's why nobody found her. Her body's down there in the dark, but her spirit made contact with me. She's trying to tell me what happened. Ted Peters must have killed her and she wants revenge. She's possessed me."

"Maddy, you don't really believe that, do you?"

"Yes! No! I don't know. Look – she had a sister called Angela. She's still alive. I need to see her. Will you come?"

"Yes, but I'm worried about you."

"So am I," Maddy said. "But I need to do it."

Angela Nielsen's home was a little cottage in Drury.

"Hi!" Maddy said to the grey-haired woman who answered the door. "Are you Angela Nielson?"

"Yes?" the woman said suspiciously. "How can I help you?"

Maddy and Izzy formed a plan before arriving. They pretended to be journalists writing a story about Angela's missing sister for a crime blog. Maddy hated lying, but it was easier than explaining the truth, that she thought Maureen had possessed her after a near-death experience. Angela seemed pleased to have two strangers visiting her to talk about her missing sister.

"Come in, please. I'll make some coffee, then you can ask me anything."

The coffee was too strong, but Maddy sipped it with a smile. "What can you tell us about your sister?"

"Maureen was a lovely, sweet girl – but she was bullied a lot in high school because she was overweight. I remember her being so unhappy because the popular girls called her Miss Piggy. No boys liked her. There was only one boy who did – and that was only *after* she started swimming to lose weight. She was dating him when she disappeared. His name was Tad Peters."

"Was he a suspect?"

"The police questioned him, but he claimed he'd been driving around in his Gremlin with his friends. They said they didn't see Maureen."

"What do you believe?"

"I never liked Tad. He was using her."

"Using her for what?"

"What do you think?"

"Oh. *That*."

"Yes."

"So, what do you think happened?"

"Tad killed her. Unfortunately, I have no proof."

That night Maddy had a dream of a hot summer day in 1972. Maureen was in a car with Tad and his teenage friends. They were all drinking beers and smoking weed. They stopped on the south side of Lake Kachika.

For hours they drank beers and got high, laughing and having a good time. Next, Tad persuaded her to strip for his friends. She didn't like revealing her naked body, but she did it to please him. Tad's mood changed then. He started calling her nasty names and making piggy noises. His friends joined in. Maureen cried.

As a final humiliation, Tad and his friends grabbed her clothes and drove off in his Gremlin, leaving her naked and alone.

She waited hours for them to come back, but they never did.

It was too far to walk home – but she could take a shortcut across the lake. There was a summerhouse on the other side, where some hippies lived. They would give her clothes and drive her home. She set off swimming.

Ahead, some little boys were on the shore, skipping stones. They saw her coming. She hoped they'd help. They didn't. For laughs, they started throwing stones at her. One stone smacked her in the forehead, drawing blood, and the kids ran off, leaving her to drown.

When Maddy opened her eyes, she understood *everything*.

For decades, Maureen's soul had been tormented and lost. After fifty years, only her skeleton would remain, but at least Maureen could find some peace if Maddy hired a diver to search and recover her bones.

That was all Maureen wanted now. Burial and final rest. Not revenge.

Feeling lighter, Maddy walked outside and stopped at the water's edge, saying goodbye to the girl in the lake.

THE BLACK ROOM

Some people think I married Madison for her money. They see me – a penniless cliché of a struggling artist, a *very* handsome man less than a third of her age – and assume that I admired her bank accounts and investments portfolio. They think I'm a gold-digger using her as my personal cash machine – but they are wrong. I didn't marry Madison for her money. I married her for her *art*. More specifically: her private collection of Janko paintings, which she kept in her vault inside her mansion and never showed to anyone. Anyone except me. She gave me that privilege once I was her husband. It was worth marrying the old bag just to see her Janko paintings. They are, without any doubt, a work of astounding genius.

There are also the reason why I must murder my wife tonight.

Five years ago, back in art college in Dublin, I had heard nothing about Janko. His work was not even in the footnotes of the art books I had read. After graduating, I heard about him at a gallery opening in New York attended by a load of rich widows looking to patronise starving young artists like me. The women all had first names that sounded like street addresses - Madison, Chelsea, Sutton and Brooklyn. I was there for the free buffet and alcohol, drinking Krug champagne and eating beluga caviare. The rich women around me ummed and aahed over the paintings on display. The old socialites looked like a group of witches with their botoxed faces frozen in creepy smiles, their flesh nip/tucked in an attempt to make themselves look younger. I hated every one of them and opted to spend my time trying to seduce a hot nineteen-year-old blonde serving the drinks. The blonde was unfortunately too dedicated to keeping her job to fall for my line of blarney. She smiled and walked away, making me feel like I was losing my luck.

"Give it up," a voice said behind me. "She's too smart to be interested in you, Sean."

"Elias. Wondered where you'd gone. Is that coke on your nose?"

Elias rubbed his nose and slipped his hand over my shoulder. "Yeah – I needed it. I just made out with a rich woman in the bathroom. She had her sixty-year-old tongue in my mouth. It tasted like cold rancid ham."

"Ugh, mate. I did not want to know that."

Elias grabbed a glass of champagne and drank it like a mouthwash. "I feel used, dude. If I didn't need the money -"

"But you do need the money, right?"

"Damn straight, I need the money, bro. God. Look at them. The billionaire widows. They're hideous. But they are so loaded it is unreal. I just sold one of my paintings for the price of a car. You sold anything, bro?"

"Not yet," I said. None of my paintings had a green SOLD sticker. I'd been at the party for three boring hours. It looked like nothing would sell.

"You know your problem, Sean?"

"No – what?"

"You aren't selling yourself, dude. It's all about the artist, not the art. You think people invest in what they see on the canvas? No way. A million people can paint expertly – but only a select few become successful. Want to know why? They have to be chosen by the small community of rich investors. They have to like you, then you're made. You know what you need?"

"No – but I'm sure you're going to tell me."

"You need to get someone to back you. I think you should try talking to that old lady over there wearing the short black dress and diamond necklace. She's been checking you out since you came in. Her name's Madison Du Vermer. They say she outbid everyone at Sotheby's for a collection of Janko originals."

I guessed I was supposed to be impressed. "Janko?"

"What? You haven't heard of Janko?"

"No," I admitted.

"Janko is incredible. They have one of his paintings in the Museum of Modern Art. Go see it tomorrow – it will blow your mind – but right now go over there with me and I'll introduce you to Madison. If you make a sale, I'd like you to remember you owe me, bro. Be charming. Get her to like you and you never know what will happen."

I sighed. I wanted another drink before going over – but Elias was already moving across the gallery, dragging me with him through the crowd.

"Madison! This is Sean Sharkey. He's a talented artist from Ireland."

Elias patted me hard on the back and excused himself, leaving me to make conversation with a woman older than my nana back in County Down. She smiled like a cadaver and asked me to show her my work. That was something I wanted to do if it would help me sell something – so I forced a smile as I showed her my favourite piece, *Quiet Before The Mass*. It was a brilliant piece and I expected her to love it – or at least *say* she loved it – but she nodded and dismissed it with barely a glance.

"That's nice," she said, which meant she thought it was rubbish.

Okay. I could deal with that. I had more paintings. I showed her another. The same bored reaction. And another. I turned on the charm, hoping my Colin Farrell looks would soften her opinion. All night I flirted with her shamelessly – but she was a wily old bird. She said she was interested in seeing all of my paintings – but she did not buy any. "You have a great eye, Sean. A huge talent. But these pieces do not quite do it for me. Are you working on anything new?"

"Yes," I said. "I have some experimental paintings in my studio. They are abstracts, radically different from these works. They are not finished, though. But I'm confident you will like them. Would you like to see them when they are done?"

I felt like a hungry puppy begging for scraps from his mistress' dining table.

"I'll give you my number," she said, removing a gold business card from within her Mulberry clutch bag. "Call me if you want me to have a look. It's been a pleasure meeting you, Sean. I have to leave now for dinner. Have a good evening. Good night."

I accepted her business card and watched her leave with a silver-haired older man in a tux who must have been her date for the evening. What? She was rejecting me for him? Angrily, I crumpled up the card and threw it into a waste bin and walked away, but then I had second thoughts. Madison had rejected my work – but she had not rejected me. Maybe I could get her to buy something if we met again? I would have to finish my latest work first. Since she liked buying the work of Janko, I decided I would find out more about him in the morning. Then I could produce something similar she would buy. Hating myself for wanting her patronage so much that I was willing to compromise my art, I retrieved her business card and slipped it into my wallet.

The whole evening would have been a complete waste of my time – except the blonde was waiting for me when I left. She was leaning against the building, flicking through pictures of her phone, her short skirt and long legs drawing my eyes. She looked up and licked her lips.

"Hello, again," she said. "I couldn't show I was interested at work - but I'm free now. I love an Irish accent. It's very sexy. I'm bored. Want to go to a club?"

"No," I said, taking pleasure in seeing her surprised and wounded expression. I waited for a second, then added with a devilish grin: "Let's go to your place right now."

"Okay," she said.

I didn't ask her name. We had a good time at her apartment. A very good time. I left before she woke up the next morning and went straight home to my studio in Greenwich Village. I lived in it with five other people because I could not afford to rent my own place. I was months behind on my share of the rent – so I sneaked in and avoided them. I showered and changed, then sneaked back out to visit the Museum of Modern Art.

The Janko painting was on a wall on its own. From a distance, it looked like a large and featureless blue square. I was unimpressed. Elias had said it would blow my mind – but it was just a blue square. It was entitled Cool Blue #4. I stood in front of it and stared at it from a dozen angles.

Someone walked up to me. "What do you think?"

The questioner was an Asian girl with short-cropped white hair that poked up at a dozen angles like a spiky crown. She was wearing a black leather miniskirt and a pink tank top. Her perfectly symmetrical features made her very beautiful. She was waiting for me to reply.

"It's blue," I said. "Very blue."

"Is that all? Do you see anything else?"

"No," I admitted. "Do you see something more?"

"Sometimes, yes. You have to look at it from the corner of your eye. Look ahead at the centre – but really concentrate on your peripheral vision. Just stare without blinking. Focus on the edges of what you can see."

She stood beside me and we stared at the blue square. I saw

nothing immediately – but by focusing on my peripheral vision I detected subtleties. The painting was not one shade of blue. There were many shades. And those shades hid something. A secret picture only visible after staring at it for several minutes. Then – suddenly – I could see more colours and focus on what was secretly painted beneath the blue.

"Oh, wow! I see a young woman in a room. She's naked and standing by an open window looking out at the sea. She looks sad. I can feel the cool breeze on my face from the window and hear the waves lapping against the shore. It's -" I blinked and lost it. It was just a blue square again. "God. How is that done? I felt like I was there in the room with her. I felt the cool air."

"I know," the girl said. "Isn't it amazing?"

I nodded. "Is it an optical illusion?"

"Nobody knows how he did it. That's Janko's secret. He called it 'sensory extra perception' and used it in all of his Red, White and Blue series."

"It's incredible. Who is the woman?"

"She was his lover at the time. Madison Something."

"Madison Du Vermer?"

"Yes – that's right. How did you know?"

"I met her last night at a gallery showing my work. I heard she owned some Jankos – so I decided to see this one."

"You're an artist! That's so exciting. I love art – but I can't do it. I write instead. Anyone can do that! I'm hoping to finish a novel by the time I leave NYU. That's *my* aim, anyway. My parents want me to be a lawyer. Are you a student, too?"

"No – I got my degree in 2013. Now I'm just a struggling artist. My name's Sean. Sean Sharkey. You won't have heard of me."

"I'm Yuko."

I invited Yuko for lunch. I didn't have the money for anything fancy – so we ate hot dogs in Central Park. I had an idea then, one inspired by Janko. "I'd like to paint you in Janko's style. Would you come back to my studio to model for me?"

She frowned. "I don't know. You could be a serial killer."

"Do I look like one?"

"Well ... no."

"I'd love to paint you. You're beautiful."

She blushed. "Would I have to be naked?"

"No," I said. "Not unless you want to be."

"Then okay!"

Luckily, my flatmates were out when we arrived. Yuko posed on a couch fully clothed and I set up a new canvas on my easel. I took some reference photos and sketched her in charcoals before mixing some oil paints. Wanting to emulate the style of Janko, I concentrated on using my peripheral vision as I painted just in shades of blue. I wanted to create a subtle masterpiece like Cool Blue #4. I worked for hours just trying to get the shades right. My eyes ached by the time I heard one of my flatmates jiggling a key in the door. I stopped painting and looked at my work. The result was less than satisfactory. In fact, it was terrible – like a painting created by a blind monkey. Yuko wanted to look at it – but I covered it with a sheet and told her I'd let her see it only after I completed it.

She looked disappointed. "Come on! Show me!"

"Not yet. You wouldn't let someone read your first draft, would you? You wouldn't want them to see your typos and mistakes?"

"I suppose not," she said, pouting. "But you will show me when it's done?"

"I'll call you," I said. "Give me your digits."

As soon as Yuko had gone, my flatmate ripped off the sheet and laughed. "Jeez, Sean, this is bad. If you want that hot chick to jump your bones, you'd better come up with something better than this. This will never pay the rent you owe us."

I hated my flatmate, but he was right about the painting.

I needed to make it better.

To do that, I needed to know more about Janko's technique if I wanted to impress Yuko *and* sell some of my paintings. That required research. My first source of information was Wikipedia. There was an article on Janko – but it was scant in details and lacked any references. The information was obviously copied from somewhere else – but where? All the article told me was a brief biography.

Kane Richard Janko was born in New York in 1930. He was an abstract painter at the New York School, producing works like Jackson Pollock until he developed his own technique 'sensory extra-perception paintings' around 1950. His first collection was shown at the Betty Parsons Gallery in 1952. It was called the Red series. His second collection – the White series – was shown in 1956. Never as successful as his contemporaries, he stopped painting after his Blue series was shown in 1965. The critics mauled it for being derivative of his early work. He was rumoured to have given up art after that, retiring to the Hamptons with his wife Madison, the inspiration for his Blue series. Shockingly, he had died in 1978 from a self-inflicted gunshot wound. He blew off his head with a shotgun inside his studio, leaving his widow his entire collection. She had sold a few of his paintings that were now worth millions each – but most of his work still belonged to her.

There was nothing else on Wikipedia – so I did some Google searching. I found the original source of the information eventually – an obituary written for the New York Times - but it provided no more detail. After more research, I was frustrated to learn nobody in the art world knew how to replicate his 'sensory extra-perception' technique.

There was only one person I knew who might – his wife and muse, Madison Du Vermer.

I took the crumpled card out of my pocket and phoned her number. A young woman answered with a German accent. She was Madison Du Vermer's personal assistant Gretchen. I explained why I was calling. She arranged for me to see her employer the next day at her home in the Hamptons.

"Uh – I don't have a car." *Or the money for a cab.* "Can she …?"

"She'll send her driver to pick you up at seven," Gretchen said. "Be ready then. Miss Du Vermer does not like tardiness. She is a very busy woman."

Madison's mansion looked like a castle from Eastern Europe made of almost-luminous white marble. Her assistant was waiting for me at the grand entrance. She was a platinum blonde beauty with high cheekbones and a haughty demeanour. She looked at me coldly. "Miss Du Vermer is having tea by the pool. Please follow me, Mr Sharkey."

We went through an archway into a beautiful garden. Her employer was next to a pool reclining on a sun lounger, wearing a figure-hugging white swimsuit that would have looked sexy on a woman in her twenties. On a woman her age, it looked horrific. Too much pasty white flesh was exposed – wrinkled and flabby – making her look like a giant slug drying out in the sun. Gretchen turned on her heels and left us alone. There was another sun lounger – but I didn't take it. I was very uncomfortable. I wanted to throw a towel over her.

"Sit down," Madison said, turning her eyes upon me. They were a raptor's eyes, the eyes of a predator studying its prey. "So, you want to know more about my husband's art, Sean?"

"Yes," I said. "I saw Blue #4. I could see you in it." *As a much younger and prettier woman.* "I was hoping to learn his technique since you posed for him and saw him working. I want to improve my art with your help."

She smiled. "You want me to tell you his secret?"

"Very much," I said.

"You must prove yourself worthy. Hand me my robe, darling. Then I'll show you something special."

We went into the castle/mansion and to a cavernous white room filled with white paintings, lit by sunlight pouring through a skylight.

The effect of so much white paint and white sunlight was blinding. I blinked tears as I entered until my eyes adjusted.

"This is my husband's entire White collection. Study it. Come to me when you have seen them all. If you can tell me what is hidden in them, I will tutor you."

She closed the door behind me. I moved to the middle of the room and concentrated. Blank whiteness surrounded me for a long time. I was convinced there was nothing else – but then my eyes detected a flickering and all became clear. Butterflies. He had painted thousands and thousands of butterflies. They looked so real I could feel their gentle wings moving the air around me, caressing my skin.

And then I blinked and they were gone.

I found Madison in another room with Gretchen. She was talking on her phone when I walked in. "Sell it and transfer the money into tech stock. Yes – today." She ended her call and turned to me. "Well, what did you see?"

"Butterflies."

"How many?"

"Thousands."

"Count them and come to me again."

I returned to the white room. I looked again. The butterflies returned. It seemed like an impossible task counting them – but I did not leave the room for several hours. My eyes were sore and my head throbbed – but I had an answer.

"5672."

"Maybe you are worthy," she said. "Very well. Starting tomorrow, I will teach you my husband's technique. But I can't have you living so far away in New York. You must move in here. Gretchen will help you transfer your belongings. You can have a suite in the west wing and use my husband's old studio."

I didn't want to move in with an old woman, even if she owned an enormous mansion. I had concerns. "How long will it take to learn his technique?"

"Several months."

"There's a little problem. I owe some rent."

"Do not worry about that, Sean. Gretchen will pay off your debts."

"Thanks. How can I thank you?"

"Thank me by working hard, Sean."

"I will. I promise."

Gretchen arranged for a moving company to empty my room of my meagre belongings. My flatmates looked very happy to receive a cheque for my rent. They also seemed pleased to see me leave.

"How long have you worked for Madison?" I asked Gretchen on our way back to the Hamptons in a limo.

"I do not work for her exactly," she said. "I am her stepdaughter. She married my father after Janko died. He was a billionaire. She inherited his entire estate after he died in 2002. She *kindly* let me stay on as her personal assistant and allows me to live in the house my father used to own."

Her tone suggested she was not happy with the situation. I wouldn't have been either if my dad had married someone and given away his fortune. Luckily for me, my dad was as poor as me. Gretchen had to be unhappy.

"You don't like her, do you?"

"Do you?" she countered.

"She is ... demanding."

"You have no idea," Gretchen said.

Over the next few weeks, I barely saw Madison. She told me to study Janko's paintings in the three rooms she had built especially for them – The Red Room, The Blue Room and The White Room – and promised to tell me how he had done them when she was not busy.

I grew obsessed with Janko's work, which revealed new depths every time I studied them. I tried to replicate his intricate brushwork in his studio, but nothing I did came close to his work.

One day Gretchen came into the studio while I was working. She looked bemused. "You really have no idea how to do it."

"She promised to teach me – but I haven't seen her in days."

"You need to show her you're interested."

"I am interested! I study the paintings every day!"

"Not the paintings. Her. Show her you're interested in her. She was once a very beautiful woman adored for her looks. That made her vain. She wants *you* to be attracted to her."

I grimaced. "She's over seventy."

"That doesn't stop her from wanting a handsome young man like you. That's why she invited you here – not for your skills with an art brush. Make her think you are interested in her. Make her fall in love. Then make her marry you."

"Why would *you* want that?"

"She's getting older. She'll die in a few years. At the moment all of her money – my father's money – goes to a charity. But if she falls in love with you … You could make her change her will. I'll help you seduce her – if you promise to give me half of everything later. You can have the art and I'll have the house. What do you say? Do we have a deal?"

I should have said no – but I wanted the art. Fine art is like fine wine. It is rare and not affordable to ordinary people. Only the rich can possess it.

"Yes," I said. "We have a deal. What do we do? How do I seduce her – with Werther's Originals?"

"Take off your shirt when you're painting," she said. "Let her see your muscles the next time she visits the studio. Act sexier. Be interested in everything she says. Hang on to her words like they are sweet music to your ears. Don't talk about Janko. Talk about *her*. Seduce her subtly. I know you can do it. I have faith in you."

I felt like a gigolo when I stripped off my shirt – but it worked on Madison. The old witch was practically salivating when she saw my chest covered in sweat as I worked feverishly at my easel.

"What are you painting?" she said.

"You," I said.

I had found an old photograph of her when she was gorgeous. I'd copied it. It wasn't my best work – but she liked it. "Oh - I looked so beautiful when I was younger."

"You still do," I said. "Why don't you pose for me now?"

We married six months later. No pre-nup. Madison was so in love with me that she changed her will to make me her sole beneficiary. I had done everything necessary to make her believe I loved her and craved her wizened body, while having an affair with her stepdaughter. Gretchen also believed I loved her – but I did not love her either. I loved Yuko. I was seeing her behind Madison and Gretchen's backs whenever I went to New York. (Yuko had no idea I was involved with anyone else.) I needed Gretchen to stay on my side until the old woman died – but I had no intention of sharing my inheritance with her. I planned to kick her out as soon as the crone was six feet under. I just had to wait and let time do its work for me.

After the hideous nightmare that was our honeymoon, Madison brought up the subject of Janko. "Darling, I think it is time I showed you the secret of his work. Come with me to the vault."

Madison's wine cellar was down a long flight of stairs. There was a steel door at the back of it, lurking in a shadowy archway. I had not known it existed. She unlocked it with a key. "My second husband kept his valuable documents in here. It's climate-controlled to keep everything from decaying. I put my husband's secret in here."

I stepped into a brick-lined corridor. Lights came on slowly as the steel door closed automatically behind us. Madison led the way to a second door. It was also locked. She unlocked it with another key. The room inside looked like a bank vault with rows of steel boxes on one wall. Madison opened a box numbered 203.

"This is my husband's secret."

There was a strange contraption inside the box, shaped like a pair of swimming goggles. They looked crudely constructed from sharp metal and jagged fragments of glass turned into bizarre lenses. The goggles had a leather strap for attaching to the wearer's head – but nobody in their right mind would do that.

"What's that?" I said,

"My husband called it an ocular receptor. It was made by Sir Isaac Newton. He found it in a junk shop in Prague when he was seventeen. Newton spent many years studying optics, including experimenting on his own eyes. He once poked his eye out of its socket to better understand how it worked. Not something I would recommend. This device was his last invention. Nobody knows it exists except for you and me. My husband used it to make his paintings. Put them on and see what he saw."

The ocular receptor looked like it would hurt if I strapped it on – but curiosity got the better of me. I attached it to my head. The goggles snapped over my eyes and the sharp metal points pinned back my eyelids. I felt a stabbing pain.

"God! It's hurting me!"

"Don't panic, darling. I need to make some adjustments to the screws."

Madison twisted something on one side. The metal creaked as the device tightened on my head. The lenses – made into the shape of a lemon squeezer – touched my corneas. I saw flashes and colours. There was a dark spot directly in front of me where the lenses were pressing into my eyes – but around them I saw seeing more colours than I had ever imagined. There was more pain at first – but it faded away as I adapted to it. I felt like I was looking through a kaleidoscope into a whole new world.

"How does it work?"

"It makes you see with your peripheral vision more clearly, expanding the spectrum. My husband wore them when he was painting. It made it possible for him to record not just the colours of images – but the memory of those things. If you keep them on, it will make it much easier for you to see his work. You won't have to concentrate at all. Darling, I'd like to show you what he was working on in the few months before he died. Take my hand and I'll show you the way."

We left the vault and walked down the corridor to another room. She unlocked it and guided me into a dark space.

"My late husband was working on a new collection when he died. The Black series. I keep them here. Welcome to the Black Room."

She stood behind me while I looked into the darkness. The ocular receptor revealed the walls were adorned with paintings. Black paintings. At least they would have looked black if I had not been wearing the weird goggles. I could see the details instantly, despite the darkness. Each painting was of an attractive dark-haired girl in a large hotel bedroom. The pictures were sensuous and intimate and obviously painted by a lover.

"That's Sophia. She was my maid. My beloved husband cheated on me with her and had the audacity to paint her picture, thinking I would never put on his horrible-looking device and see his betrayal. But I did. One day I went into his studio and crept up behind him. He was wearing the ocular receptor. He didn't hear me until I started tightening the screws, driving the lenses into his eyes. He died screaming. Afterwards, I used a shotgun to disguise what had really happened. I got away with murdering him – just like I'll get away with hurting you."

"What?" I said.

Her fingers were suddenly tightening the screws, drawing the lenses into my pupils. The pain was intense. I could feel the pressure on my eyes and yelled out when the sharp glass sliced my pupils and unleashed hot aqueous humour down my cheeks. I fell to my knees in agony and desperately pulled at the evil device. I ripped it off, hearing my crazy wife laughing. She was somewhere nearby – but I could not see her.

"You've blinded me!"

"It's the least I could do, darling. Did you really think I would not find out if you cheated on me? I had a detective follow you since we began dating. I know all about Gretchen and that other girl. I'm going to punish them too – but first I'm going to leave you in here for a while with my late husband's paintings. They are quite brilliant, though I doubt you'll appreciate them now."

She locked me in.

*

That was several hours ago. For a long time, I whimpered on the floor in absolute agony – blind and bleeding.

To stop the blood loss, I bandaged my ruined eyes with the sleeve from my shirt – but there's still blood seeping through. The pain of losing my eyes is the worst thing I have ever endured.

Hoping someone would hear me, I screamed and banged on the walls – but the vault was too deep and too thick-walled. I have no choice but to wait for Madison to come back.

I can't see a thing – but I've made the ocular receptor into a sort of weapon.

Now, I'm listening for her return.

I know I'll only get one chance to attack her when she opens the door – but I've got to take it.

There's a noise outside.

Footsteps.

She's coming.

I sigh and prepare myself behind the door.

I know what I must do.

I must murder my wife tonight.

THE SKELETON

Melanie promised to be our designated driver before we drove to her cousin's Halloween party in Brighton – but she started drinking the near-lethal punch sometime during the evening without telling me first. I found out how drunk my wife was after I'd already had a few pints of Stella.

By then, Melanie was dancing drunkenly to Miley Cyrus's *Wrecking Ball*. She was dressed as Catwoman, looking very sexy in tight black rubber and a mask. She was twerking with one of her girlfriends, wearing a slutty vampire costume, drawing the attention of every man in the room. Some were capturing her erotic dancing on their phones. Tomorrow videos of my wife would be on Facebook and Instagram. Embarrassed for her, I pushed through the crowd of hot bodies until I reached her. I felt like an idiot wearing my Batman costume – but I was glad we were both disguised. My wife was a solicitor. If her partners in her firm saw her behaving like a drunken teenager, she could lose her job at Mariot Hartley. "Mel, stop that. You're making a scene."

"Hey, Batman!" she said, continuing to twerk. "Let's dance!"

She turned her back on me and started shaking her bottom so wildly that she lost her balance and stumbled into the other dancers. She would have tripped over her own feet if I had not grabbed her and pulled her away from the dance floor. She giggled and hummed the tune, mumbling some of the words, slurring most of them. I glared at her when we were out of the crowd.

"You promised to stay sober!" I said over the loud music. "You look wasted, Mel."

"What? Oh! Yeah. Shhoow shorry. I've had a little bit of punchy-wunchy. That stuff's really, really strong. Think it's got rum *and* vodka in it. Ka-pow! Zap! Blammo!"

She laughed and tried to make me dance – but I was not in the mood. "Mel, you've not had a *little* drink. You've had a whole bowlful. What were you *thinking*?"

She frowned. "Are you mad at me, Eric?"

"Yes!"

"Why?"

"I'm going to have to stop drinking now. I'll have to drive us home – even though you promised you'd do that."

"Whoops!" she said. "Sorry."

She giggled and grinned. She was not sorry at all. She had got herself drunk so I, her dutiful husband, would have to be responsible and stay sober while she had all the fun. Her plan was so transparent that I was angry at myself for believing her earlier. For the rest of the night, I stayed off the booze so she could enjoy herself – but I resented her trickery. If Melanie had wanted me to be the designated driver, she should have been honest and said so. But she had known I would not have wanted to go to her cousin's party if I couldn't drink. I would have preferred to stay in watching TV. To make me drive to Brighton, she had lied. I sighed. She didn't have to play games. We were supposed to be mature adults.

At midnight, I guided my inebriated wife to our car. Melanie could barely keep her eyes open. I lifted her into the passenger seat and strapped her in. As I hurried around to the driver's side, she slumped into unconsciousness.

I started driving us back to our home.

We were almost there when something weird happened. I was on a suburban street about fifteen miles from our house when a skeleton ran across the road straight into my path.

For a moment I thought I was dreaming – until I realised it was a kid in a Halloween costume. It looked like a small boy aged about eight or nine. He was running and not looking for cars – just like I had not been looking for a kid out after midnight. I had remembered it was Halloween – but I had never thought any young children would still be running around when I drove back from the party. The skeleton dashed out from between two parked cars as I was passing at forty-something miles per hour, giving me no time to avoid hitting him. I heard a sickening, wet thump on impact. I slammed on my brakes after I had smashed into him. His little body bounced off my car and flew into some rose bushes in the front garden of a semi-detached house on the street corner.

I stopped and shuddered. My heart punched my ribs as I stared at what I had done. Beside me, my wife remained unconscious, blissfully unaware. I shook her – but she didn't wake up.

"Hell," I muttered.

What was I going to do?

I looked at the skeleton in the rose bushes. The boy's arms and legs were broken and twisted, leaving me in no doubt that he was very badly hurt. His wet blood flowed down his chest as the kid twitched like someone having an epileptic fit.

He was still alive – so I could save him!

I opened my door, feeling the frigid night air strike my face. It was the coldness that sobered me. I wasn't drunk when I hit the kid – but I had been drinking a few beers at the party. As I rushed over to the boy, I started feeling worried for myself in case anyone had seen the accident and called the police. There's a difference between having a few social drinks and being drunk – but I doubted the police would take that into consideration if they tested my blood for alcohol. They'd blame me for the accident even though I could not have avoided hitting him, drunk or sober. That fear made me slow down before I got to the bushes. I looked around for witnesses. The houses were dark. I prayed nobody was looking out. No other cars were coming in either direction – but I was frightened that someone would drive by and see me.

From ten feet away, I could see the boy's blood had stopped flowing. He was no longer twitching. Motionless and silent, he definitely wasn't breathing. Several thorns had slashed his costume, tearing his flesh. The wounds were horrible. Bile rose in my throat. I looked away.

Quickly, I approached the boy. I felt for a pulse in his neck. Nothing. I didn't need to be a doctor to know what that meant. He was dead. I felt sick. I had killed a little boy. There was nothing I could do now for him – but I could save myself from going to prison if I GOT OUT OF THERE before anyone saw me.

Hating myself, I ran back to my car. Melanie was sitting up. Her eyes were open. I thought she had seen the boy, but her eyes were unfocused.

"Are we home?" she said.

"Not yet," I said.

"Wake me when we get there," she said, closing her eyes again. "God, I'm so drunk ..."

I turned on the engine and drove off.

I only looked back once to check nobody was following me.

It looked like I had got away with it.

There were no witnesses – thank God.

I didn't feel relieved, though.

I was a hit-and-run driver.

I hated people like that.

They were scum.

I was scum too now.

I was a criminal.

What now?

It was good nobody had witnessed the accident – but there was plenty of forensic evidence linking my vehicle to the boy's death. His blood and skin were all over the front of my car. I had seen the gore before I got back in. I should have taken a minute to wipe it down with a cloth – but I'd thought it was more important to get away from the crime scene. I drove about a quarter of a mile and then pulled over. I used a rag kept in the glove compartment to clean the blood off the bumper and bonnet. The rag was soaked in blood when I had finished. I wanted to toss it in a bin somewhere – but what someone found it? For now, I wrapped the bloody rag inside a plastic carrier bag in the boot. I'd get rid of it later. My wife was snoring softly when I drove on.

I wanted to go home – but I couldn't get the thought of the dead boy out of my head. I couldn't leave his corpse where it was. Somebody would find it in the morning, then the police would know it had been a hit-and-run. It was better – safer – to make his body disappear completely. At least then the cops would not be looking for a driver. They'd probably think some local creep had abducted him. It would make it harder for them to figure out what happened if they didn't have a body to examine.

I drove back to the scene of the accident, fearing someone would have already discovered the dead boy.

Luckily, the street was the same as before.

Nobody was around. The night was cold and dark and silent.

Leaving my wife asleep, I got out and opened the boot. Quickly, before I had a chance to change my mind, I hurried over to the rose bushes and picked up the lifeless skeleton. The boy weighed almost nothing. I carried him to my car. He was so small he fitted easily inside. I closed the boot, then raced around to the driver's side.

I drove off again, this time with a corpse in the boot.

Had I done the right thing or made everything a million times worse?

It was bad *accidentally* killing a kid – but moving the body from the scene?

There was no excuse for that.

A jury would sentence me to the maximum.

We were only ten miles from our home, but it felt like an epic journey across a dozen continents. I wanted to get there quickly – but I didn't want to get caught speeding. I drove well under the speed limit.

Going home that night was the longest, most stressful journey of my life. Every second I expected a police car to flash its lights and pull me over. I was stunned when I made it home without incident.

At two o'clock, I parked my car on our driveway, too shocked by what I had done to think straight. All I could think of was the sight of the skeleton in the rose bushes. My wife was stirring – so lifted her out and helped her walk into our house. She passed out again on our sofa. I carried her up the stairs to our bedroom. She woke briefly on the landing, smiled at me and said she loved me, then closed her eyes. She was snoring two minutes later. I was pretty sure she wouldn't wake up for several hours. That was good. It gave me time to clean up my car and get rid of the body.

I stripped off my Batman costume to put on some jeans and a T-shirt. I returned to the car and moved it into our garage, where I inspected it under the bright artificial light. I could see loads of places where I'd missed with the rag. There was brown hair stuck to the licence plate. Wearing gloves, I plucked it off and put it into a bag. Then I hosed down my car from bumper to bumper. That wasn't good enough, so I filled a bucket with soapy water and scrubbed it thoroughly. I worked for hours getting it clean. I removed all traces of the accident that were visible and – hopefully – everything that wasn't. There were dents and scratches that I could not do anything about – but they were not obvious. You needed to study the bodywork closely to see them.

Exhausted, I put everything I had used into a bin liner inside another bin liner. I would dump that in the morning on my way to work. I prayed I had removed all visible traces of evidence – but I was still worried because I had not dealt with the biggest problem, the corpse in the boot.

In the harsh light, I stood beside the boot, afraid of looking in. I didn't want to look at the kid again. But I couldn't leave him in there for long. He would decompose, making my car stink. I had to dump him somewhere before he rotted into a gooey mess. There was some woodland about a mile away or a lake or the river – but I didn't fancy dumping a body in the dark. I'd be better off waiting for daylight, so I wouldn't make a mistake. I couldn't get rid of him before cleaning him of forensic evidence, anyway. The impact would have left trace evidence on the boy. I had watched so many episodes of CSI and Bones to know that the tiniest trace of evidence could convict someone. I would have to clean the body before dumping it. I laid down some plastic sheeting, then looked for some bleach in the kitchen.

Bleach was excellent at destroying DNA. I grabbed every bottle under the sink and returned to the garage.

That was when I heard the noise.

A scratching sound.

Coming from inside the boot.

I froze. Listening.

The scratching continued.

What the hell was going on?

I'd been sure the boy was dead – but what if I'd been wrong? I wasn't a doctor. I could have made a mistake. *Please, God, let it be a mistake. Let the boy live.*

I had to save him, even if it meant going to prison.

I dropped the bleach bottles and approached the boot, listening to the scratching, scratching, scratching. I was afraid of the boy dying before I got it open.

"I'm so sorry," I said, unlocking the boot with my electronic key. "I'll get you to a hospital. Just hold on."

I pulled on the lever to open the boot. The boot rose slowly. It was dark inside. Something moved. Something smelled foul. I knew something was very, very wrong, but I was slow to react. I wasn't expecting danger. With alarming speed, the boy in the skeleton costume leapt out, snarling like a wild animal, knocking me backwards. For a little boy, he had shocking strength. I fell onto my back on the hard concrete, with the skeleton on top of me. He was trying to scratch and bite me – but I pushed him off.

"Calm down, kid. I'm trying to help you!"

The boy snarled. I saw his malicious eyes through the skeleton mask. They looked blood red. There was no humanity present. I felt like I was in the presence of pure evil. The boy wasn't right in the head, but that was completely understandable, given the circumstances. He probably thought I was going to hurt him again. He growled like a beast and came at me like a broken-limbed spider. I was terrified. I scooted backwards to get away from him, banging into the closed garage doors. With no way of escaping, I grabbed the nearest object – a bleach bottle – and hurled it at the deranged child. The bottle struck him in the face and bounced off, doing no damage, but it knocked off his skeleton mask, exposing his face.

Underneath, his skin was grey, white and green, the colours of mouldy cheese.

No living boy looked like that.

He was dead.

Definitely dead.

Long dead.

I knew in an instant that he'd already been dead *when I'd hit him with my car*. There was no other explanation for his decayed state. I'd hit a dead boy – a real-life zombie. That was why he was wandering around alone at midnight. He must have turned into a zombie earlier in the night. I hadn't killed a living boy. I'd smashed into a member of the living dead.

I sighed with relief. I was in the beginning of a zombie apocalypse, but at least I wasn't a *murderer*.

Unfortunately, I didn't have long to feel the relief of a clear conscience.

Making an unholy growl, the zombie was coming towards me, snarling, his teeth gnashing, his dark tongue dripping saliva.

"Stop! Get away from me!"

He didn't listen. He kept crawling forwards, his jaws opening so widely I could see the back of his throat.

Making a sound like a frightened kitten, I crawled away from him. He tried to bite my feet. I kicked out, knocking him backwards. He shook his head, spitting out a broken tooth, then charged at me. I got to my feet and ran around the side of my car. There were some tools on the wall – hammers and power tools. I grabbed a big claw hammer and spun around to fight back – but the zombie kid had disappeared. I looked left and right, expecting an attack at any second. Cold sweat ran down my forehead, stinging my eyes.

Slowly, I walked around the garage, looking under the wheels. I could not see him hiding there. I could not hear him, either.

I picked up a torch from a toolbox and shone it into the shadows.

He wasn't there.

Where had he gone?

(Up. You haven't looked up.)

Nervously, I looked up. In a movie, the zombie would have been hanging from the ceiling, waiting to pounce. He wasn't.

But he had to be somewhere. He wasn't a ghost. Zombies were solid flesh. They didn't disappear. Or did they? Frankly, I wasn't too confident about my zombie knowledge. I knew what they did in horror films, but what skills did they have in real life? Could they climb? Could they turn invisible?

My heart was hurting my chest with every thud that sounded in my ears.

Where had he gone?

The garage wasn't a large space.

There were no hiding places.

That meant …

No!

The door leading into my house had a dirty handprint on it.

Hell. The zombie boy was inside with my unconscious wife. She was unaware of the danger.

I ran to the door. He'd left a bloody, sticky trail across the hallway, a slimy mix of blood and noxious body fluids. You didn't need to have a GPS to track his route. The trail went up the stairs in the direction of our bedroom, where my wife was sleeping. Vulnerable.

"MELANIE!" I shouted, running up the stairs. "MELANIE! WAKE UP! THERE'S A ZOMBIE IN OUR HOUSE!"

I reached the top of the stairs. The trail continued into our dark bedroom. I switched on a light. The zombie boy was on my bed, blocking my view of my wife. All I could see was the zombie boy's twisted body. He turned to face me, chewing something red and gooey.

Was it my wife's heart?

Rage filled me. I charged at him with the hammer raised. He snarled and lunged. I brought the hammer down hard on his head. His skull smashed like a rotting Halloween pumpkin, spraying chunks of brain tissue over the duvet and carpet.

The kid slumped and stopped moving. The hammer jutted out of his head. I let go of it, feeling sick.

This time, the zombie boy didn't come back to life.

Breathing hard, I noticed my wife wasn't in the bed.

I heard a moan behind me.

I spun around.

My wife was shuffling out of the bathroom. Her deep, guttural breathing scared the hell out of me. "Uhhhh. Uhhhh. Uhhhh."

Oh, no. Not Melanie! I grabbed the hammer and yanked it free of the dead boy's skull. Blood ran down the handle.

"Melanie?" I said.

My wife moaned again.

"Melanie, did he bite you?"

My wife didn't answer. She shuffled towards the bed. She slipped back under the duvet without opening her eyes once.

"Melanie, will you please answer me?" I approached her cautiously, hefting the hammer. "Melanie, are you all right?"

My wife groaned. "God, Eric, I just vomited everything I drank tonight. Turn out the light, please! I wanted to go back to sleep!"

Thank God she wasn't a zombie. "Mel, didn't you hear me shouting?"

"No," she mumbled. "I had my head in the toilet. Why were you shouting, anyway? What was so urgent?"

She was snuggling her face into her pillow, completely unaware of the corpse at the bottom of the bed.

"Forget it," I said. "It will wait until the morning. Go back to sleep."

"Okay," she said dreamily. Seconds later, my wife started to snore like a trucker.

I looked at the zombie's remains. Wow. It was a mess. Melanie would freak out if she woke up and saw the gore.

I was wondering if I should report the zombie to the authorities when I noticed the blood on my arm. What if it contained some kind of zombie-making virus? Got to clean it off *now*. I hurried into the bathroom and washed the blood down the sink. I scrubbed my arm with antiseptic soap. After my arm was thoroughly clean and pink with scrubbing, I noticed scratch marks on my skin from the rose bushes. The thorns had cut deeply into my flesh in several places, but I'd not felt any pain at the time. If the zombie boy had carried a virus, it was possible I'd caught it too.

I knew what I had to do then. I dragged the zombie's body into the spare bedroom and wrote a message on the door for my wife – MEL, DON'T OPEN THIS DOOR. I MIGHT BE INFECTED WITH A ZOMBIE VIRUS (THIS IS NOT A JOKE) - then locked myself inside for the night. I would sleep the night in the bed we normally reserved for guests. But first I used my phone to check on the situation.

Twitter and Facebook were on fire with news about zombie outbreaks all across Britain. Nobody knew why it was happening, but some people thought it was something to do with it being Halloween. It was crazy. Nobody knew if the undead were rising from their graves or if a virus had turned the living into the evil dead. They didn't know if it was a natural or a supernatural event. It didn't matter *why*, though. It was happening, so I had to do something to help other people before it was too late.

I called my friends and family, waking them and warning them about the situation. They didn't believe me – at first. But they did when they looked at their televisions and saw the pictures of zombies in the streets of London, Manchester and Glasgow. After twenty minutes, my internet connection crashed and I was left alone in silence, hoping they would survive the night, fearing they would not.

My arm was itching terribly. I was scared, very scared. Was I infected? Was I turning into an undead monster like the boy? I hated the uncertainty. Earlier, I'd been selfishly worried about saving myself from going to prison, but that seemed irrelevant now. Maybe Melanie would be safe if I turned into a zombie while locked up – as long as she didn't think my message was a sick joke and open the door. If I was alive and human in the morning, I'd unlock the door and break the news about the zombie apocalypse to Melanie while she nursed a killer hangover, wishing I really was Batman and she really was Catwoman. With a zombie apocalypse dawning, we needed superheroes.

Weary beyond measure, I closed my eyes, praying I'd make it through the night.

I woke up hearing knocking at the bedroom door. Bright sunlight was coming through the curtains, though it felt like only seconds since I'd gone to sleep. The zombie apocalypse. Had that all been a nightmare?

Sitting up, I realised I was in the spare bedroom. That hadn't been a dream. I checked out my arms. They were scratched, but the marks had faded. I was healing. Yes, I'd made it.

The knocking continued. Melanie! I jumped up and unlocked the door, never happier to see my wife.

Melanie was standing on the other side, her face deathly pale. In the bright daylight, I could see a raw bite mark on her leg, where the boy had taken out a chunk of her flesh. Last night, she'd been too drunk to feel any pain. Now she snarled and lunged. Before she got me, I slammed the door in her face. She banged against it, moaning. Struggling to keep it closed, I realised something that made me weep.

I'd left the hammer in the other room.

THE MAN IN THE MIRROR

Nothing prepared Antoine for his first encounter with the book. Resting on a bed of red velvet cushions, it waited for him like a beautiful woman in a boudoir, seducing him with just a look.

"Read me," the book seemed to call out in his mind. "I am yours."

But she was not his. Not yet.

Simon Quillard owned her.

Antoine stared through the display case. The book wore nothing but an old leather belt, buckled to hide her secrets from prying eyes, which made her look almost naked. The dark leather cover was several centuries old. The book had to be a private journal of some sort since nothing was identifying the contents. Antoine wondered whose words it captured within.

Quillard was watching him, checking his reaction to it with a slight smile on his face. "She is beautiful, *oui?*"

"Yes," Antoine said. "Where did you find her?"

"A collector in Paris died last month. His relatives sold me his private collection. She was among them. Hidden and forgotten."

"How many people know you have this?"

"You are the first," Quillard said. "I thought you'd want to see her before anyone else."

"Why me?"

"Ah! Have patience!" Quillard unlocked the case and lifted the glass cover, releasing a musty odour. Only ancient books smelled so earthy, like mushrooms growing in the dark. Antoine breathed it in as Quillard slipped on gloves before lifting up the book. The collector carried it over to an oak desk once owned by Louis XIIII. He laid the book gently on the surface under the bright light of a desk lamp. Breathing heavily, Quillard unbuckled the book's strap and opened it slowly to the first page. "Antoine, you will be amazed. Sit down. Read it. Here – wear these gloves."

On the first page there was a drawing of a young man with a caption below it written in French that translated as 'the man in the mirror'. It was dated August the Third, 1554. Antoine recognised the man. He saw him every day.

"That's me!"

"Go on, Antoine. Turn the page."

The book was a diary of the author's dreams, on which the author had written copious notes every morning because he had been convinced they were important. Every page contained descriptions and sketches of things the author had dreamt – things someone born centuries ago would never have imagined. Planes. Cars. Computers. Cell phones. All drawn in meticulous detail from memory by someone long dead before Antoine was born. The author had written notes about them, guessing at their functions. Antoine turned the pages, puzzled and astounded. Many pictures were of people and events in Antoine's life. He was seeing his life as seen through the eyes of a complete stranger. He reached the last page with Quillard breathing over his shoulder.

"Look! The signature! It explains so much, solving one of the greatest mysteries."

Antoine frowned. "Who was this 'Michel du Nostre-Dame'?"

"He was Nostradamus. This is priceless. I'm rich!"

"No," Antoine said with an evil grin, his hands slipping around Quillard's throat. "I am."

DO FEAR THE REAPER

Greta's little sister crept up to her at the end of the dark tunnel, whispering too loudly. "Are they out there?"

"Shush, Mara. They might hear you."

A dust storm made it hard for Greta to see the reapers searching through the wasteland for survivors – but she had glimpsed their black armour and scythe-like weapons through the greyness. The reapers wore gas masks, giving them an insect-like appearance as if they were an alien species. In many ways, they were just that. She knew they were acting like monsters, even though they were men and women inside the black combat gear. The reapers were cleaning up the world for their masters, the war-makers hiding in their distant, deep bunkers.

A reaper was squatting on concrete rubble three hundred metres away. It was looking her way – but she didn't think it could see her in the darkness. If Greta moved, she was more likely to be detected, so she stayed still, afraid of moving, afraid of breathing.

Her sister poked her in the ribs. "Greta, please tell me what you see."

"Be quiet," she snapped. "There's a reaper hunting us. Don't say or do anything, okay?"

Greta and the reaper stayed motionless for a painfully long time. Greta felt sure the reaper knew she was there – but it made no move towards her position. Was it playing a game? Was it waiting to see if she would leave the tunnel? Why was it squatting there in the dust storm when it could have taken shelter?

The dust storm grew stronger, the wind howling through the graveyard of buildings, spitting hard grains in her eyes until her vision blurred and tears ran down her cheeks. She thought of her parents, killed in the first days of the Final War, when the bombs rained down, turning her world into dust. Soon that dust was so thick it reduced her visual range to just beyond the tunnel entrance, which was good because it worked both ways, allowing her to retreat into the tunnel without the reaper spotting her.

Greta followed her sister down the twisting maze of tunnels leading back to their home under what remained of London. They lived in a rat-infested Tube station under the ruined city, where they had gathered a few essential things from the surface to make a tent on the platform. They slipped inside the warm space. Mara lit a candle while Greta wiped her face with a damp rag, cleaning herself of radioactive dust. Then Greta opened a rusty tin of spaghetti meatballs to share. They ate them cold, huddled under thick scratchy blankets, sharing an iPod's earphones, playing some music downloaded before the apocalypse. They listened to the Blue Oyster Cult's *(Don't Fear) The Reaper*. The music lulled her sister to sleep. Greta extinguished the candle and listened to the darkness.

She heard something.

Crunching footsteps.

Just outside.

The reaper was coming.

A lantern blinded her. The reaper spoke on a radio. "Found survivors. Rescuing them now."

THE DEADLINE

I always hated being alone on the eighteenth floor late at night. At midnight, every light in the building automatically turned off except for the ones at my small cubicle, where I was working to a deadline for my boss. Surrounded by silent darkness, I often felt a frightening presence when nobody else was there as if someone was watching over my shoulder. I felt their cold breath touching my neck and smelled something sour. Each time it happened, I was too afraid to turn around to see if someone was standing behind me because I knew I was the only person there.

I was sure it was a ghost.

The next day, I asked a colleague if she had heard about anyone dying in the building. She looked around nervously before answering. "It's happened to you? You felt someone watching you, even though you were alone?"

I nodded. "What is it?"

"It's Sarah. She worked all night, every night, drinking strong coffees to keep herself alert. She worked harder than anyone. One morning they found her sitting at her desk stone-cold dead. The caffeine and stress gave her a heart attack aged twenty."

I worked late the next night. I felt a presence again. Cold breath. I stayed perfectly still, waiting for the thing, whatever it was, to go away. After a minute, the feeling went away and I dared to look around, seeing nothing. Just darkness. And the lingering smell of coffee.

I quit the next morning.

MOONLIGHT

"Be quiet," Trenton said. "Something is out there."

Everyone stopped laughing at Samson's crude jokes. We listened. I looked into the darkness outside the clearing, where I thought I saw something shining in the moonlight just for an instant. It looked like a line of knives against the blackness of the forest – but they disappeared before my eyes focussed. I grabbed my rifle and stared into the dark.

"Guys, you see that?"

"What?" Samson said. He had been almost asleep by our campfire.

"Knives."

"Knives?"

"Yeah."

Now Samson looked scared, fumbling his gun out of his holster. "Where, Andy?"

"Near the trees."

"I don't see -"

"They've gone now."

Five knives. Five Indians. Watching us. Waiting for us to let our guard down so they could sneak up and cut our throats. There were only three of us – giving them an advantage in the dark.

The moonlight was our friend. We could see them coming –

as long as those black clouds didn't hide the moon. The moonlight was shining down on the rocky ground, banishing shadows, making it impossible for them to get close without being detected. We had our rifles to fend off an attack – but we couldn't shoot what we couldn't see.

I wished we hadn't camped so close to an Indian burial ground. We were trespassing on the tribe's land, but Trenton had not cared. He had shrugged at any suggestion that it was dangerous to stay in the area. I had been worried about them right from the start. The Indians would not forgive us. They would do what they did to the last white men. They'd cut off our scalps. They'd cut off our eyelids and lips. They'd make us scream and scream until they cut off our tongues. And then they'd leave us at the edge of the forest as a warning to others. Alive – but barely human any longer.

The darkness beyond the camp was still and silent – but I trusted Trenton's hearing and my own eyes. We were definitely being watching. The question was, would they attack us during the night or let us leave in the morning? We meant them no harm. We were just on our way to Denver, passing through.

My eyes performed sneaky tricks, turning the darkness into threatening shapes - monsters, dark, hungry predators, out there, waiting for our fire to turn to embers.

I wrapped my coat around my shoulders, shivering, jumping at every crack of a twig or howl of a wolf.

A cloud was drifting across the moon. The darkness thickened. Congealed like black blood. Then the moon was gone. Darkness reigned. The night felt malevolent. Dangerous.

Trenton screamed first.

Samson was next.

I saw nothing.

Just darkness.

Something was near.
Breathing.
I fired my rifle and saw something in the flash of light.
Not five knife-wielding Indians.
No.
Five teeth. Five sabre-long teeth.
Ripping my friends to pieces.
The darkness returned.
I ran. Fast.

THE CRACK

The crack appeared overnight, splitting our driveway from the street to our garage. I called the council – but they refused to help because it was on private property. My wife Sarah peered into it. "I can't see the bottom. You think it's subsidence?"

"I'll call Tony. He's a builder."

Tony examined the crack. "That is your basic inter-dimensional rift into a Stygian abyss."

"In layman's terms?"

"An opening into hell."

"Oh, great. That'll ruin property prices. Is it safe?"

"I won't get bigger – but don't stare into it. It devours souls."

Sarah glared. "Now you tell me?"

ONE WINTER MORNING

"Come over! It is safe!"

I step on the frozen lake and slowly skate to the middle, where my wife waits. I am an amateur skater – but Anne skates around me with dazzling speed, round and round, her blades leaving circles. She stops. Then she stomps.

"Anne! Stop!"

She stomps again. Harder.

The ice cracks and those cracks spread until I am standing on a circular jigsaw of wobbling pieces.

The pieces tilt.

I fall into the icy water.

As my limbs go numb, my wife skates away, leaving me wishing I had never had an affair with her sister.

CALL OF THE SHAKOLOGOTH

Last week, I received an anonymous email message. It claimed to contain an HP Lovecraft story never published before. I normally delete messages from untrusted sources – but the email had slipped by my spam filter, making me a little curious. I'd never received a spam email on that subject – so I assumed the sender knew more about me than what I listed on Facebook and LinkedIn. I opened the email and read the short message: *Think you will find this interesting. Call me backwards if you want to see the original. 555-9603.*

Someone had sent the message anonymously from an email account I didn't recognise. The phone number looked fake because everyone knows 555 is the prefix used in TV shows. What kind of joke was this? The sender must have used a smartphone to write the message because the word 'backwards' should have been 'back'. My phone always auto-completed words incorrectly like that. I hated it.

There was a 340K attachment inside the email. The file was called lovecraftjournal.jpg. The '.jpg' meant it was a picture file. The filename intrigued me. I was a huge Lovecraft fan. I collected his first editions and wrote a blog about his books called *All Things Lovecraft*. I downloaded it onto my computer, ran a virus scan, which said it was safe, then opened it.

The picture was a photocopy of two pages from a handwritten journal. The material looked like notes on a horror story about a monstrous creature called a Shakologoth. The handwriting appeared to match HP Lovecraft's style.

Re: Shakologoth. It has no physical form, but it exists within the Stygian dreams of mankind, terrorising the dying with diabolical nightmarish visions of their inescapable fates. There are six Shakologoth sleeping under Innsmouth, awaiting the return of the Cthulhu. Of these, the Prime is the most insidious. (Why?) I shall endeavour to find out on my next visit to Innsmouth.

I read the whole sample, wondering why someone had sent me, of all people, such a strange document. It had to be a hoax because Innsmouth was just a place invented by HP Lovecraft. And yet the author wrote about it as if it were real. Not only that – but they wrote it in the style of HP Lovecraft. He loved using words like "Stygian" in his stories. Obviously, this was an elaborate hoax designed to trick me into calling that phone number, which I already knew did not exist. It seemed pointless. Why would anyone go to the trouble of sending me a fake document purporting to be by Lovecraft? It was a joke in extremely bad taste.

I sat staring at my laptop screen for an hour, looking for flaws that would prove to me it was a definite fake. HP Lovecraft was an American – so would he have used the English spelling of "endeavour" or the US version "endeavor"? And why write about Innsmouth as if he were going to visit it for real? The person behind the hoax had a bizarre sense of humour. Okay – I'd play their game just to see what happened if I called that fake phone number.

I entered 5559603 into my phone. I heard it connecting. I felt nervous until a woman's recorded voice spoke. "The number you have called does not exist."

There. An automated recording, telling me what already knew. I trashed the email and deleted the downloaded picture from my computer. Then I ran a full virus scan just in case the email had sneaked something onto my hard disk.

Being careful not to wake my sleeping wife, I went to bed.

I'm in a small grey-painted room surrounded by doctors and nurses wearing face masks. What has happened? I can't remember how I'd ended up here. Have I been in an accident? I don't feel any pain.

I'm strapped onto some kind of hospital gurney, which is next to some beeping medical equipment. I can't move a muscle — but I'm fully conscious. Someone pressed a button that tilts the gurney. My body is raised to an angle so I can see through a glass wall into another room like a small auditorium where rows of strangers are observing my operation.

They are not all strangers. I recognise a few faces — a couple of friends, my brother, his wife - but they look older than I remember, much older. My own mother is there with completely white hair, her eyes tired and ancient, wet with tears. My wife Judith is there too — but she does not look at me. She has her face buried in her hands, which are heavily veined and wrinkled. There is another man beside her, holding her hand. Who the hell is he?

There is a clock on the far wall.

It reaches twelve o'clock.

At that moment, a tall bald man in a black suit nods to another man dressed like a doctor — but I have the feeling he isn't a doctor at all. There are dark tattoos on his hands. Doctors don't have tattoos on their hands. They would never risk potential nerve damage. He is not here to make me well. I think he is here to kill me. My fear is confirmed when I see him loading a clear liquid into a syringe from a bottle marked with stark warning symbols. It is a poison. A poison he intends to give me.

This isn't an operation.

It's an execution.

The man moves closer, attaching the syringe to a drip attached to my arm. There is no expression on his face. He doesn't see me as a human. I am just an animal he had to put down. He pauses. Looks at the taller man. Waits.

The other man nods again.

I can't move – but I implore the other man to stop with my eyes, the only thing I can move. I widen them in fear. Begging. Don't do it. Don't kill me

The executioner injects the liquid into the drip.

Almost instantly my arm feels hot and then hotter and then my veins burn with hot lava. The lava spreads from my arm into my chest and head. It's like being burned alive. I scream – but no sound comes out of my mouth. Instead, my body shudders and the pain increases until it feels as though every part of me is on fire, burning from the inside out. It's a white-hot agony that I pray will end – but it only increases in intensity. Burning. Burning. Burning.

I lurched awake in my bed at home. Quickly, I realised it had been a bad dream – but a bad dream so real I could feel the heat of the poison still within my blood. For several minutes, my heart pounded hard in my chest. Afraid of returning to sleep, I crept downstairs to my computer. I had trashed the email – but it was not permanently deleted. I dragged it back to life and read it again.

Think you will find this interesting. Call me backwards if you want to see the original. 555-9603.

What if the word 'backwards' had not been an error?

I reversed the order of the numbers and called that number: 3069555.

No. Nothing.

Wait.

The email had been sent from America.

I added the prefix for America to the number.

Then I called it again.

I heard it connecting.

A man answered. "Ah – you figured out my little puzzle. Well done."

I was not amused by his game. "Who is this and why did you send me that picture?"

"My name is Silas Randolpho Urquart Smith III," he said. That name was a mouthful. It was hard to believe there had been three of them. "Mr McCullen, I sent you that picture because you are a devoted Lovecraftian. I have been following your blog for several years. I admired your work, Mr McCullen. Like you, I am a Lovecraftian. I contacted you because I knew you'd be interested in seeing what I had found, but first I wanted to test you. You passed my test, Mr McCullen. Well done."

"This is a weird way of contacting me," I said. "What do you want, Mr Smith?"

"Does the name August Derleth ring a bell?"

"Yes. August Derleth posthumously edited HP Lovecraft's manuscripts. He died years ago. What about him?"

"I found a journal written by Lovecraft among some boxes of Derleth's books sold at a recent auction. The seller didn't have a clue about the importance of the journal – but I do. It contains the truth behind the Cthulhu Mythos."

The Cthulhu Mythos was the mythology invented by HP Lovecraft. I was interested in knowing more about how it had been created – but I wasn't believing a word Silas Smith was saying. "Look, I don't know why you're telling me this. You're obviously lying. That journal is a fake like the So-called Hitler Diaries."

"I knew you would be sceptical. I'd expect nothing less. Tell me something, Mr McCullen, did you have a terrible nightmare last night?"

"Yes – but so what?"

"I knew you would. You were dying in the dream, were you not?"

"Yes. How did you know that?"

"It wasn't a nightmare. Your dream was real, Mr McCullen."

"Yeah, right."

"It was a vision of your future. Specifically, your very last moments alive."

"Bull. Dreaming about death is common. It doesn't mean it's real."

"Let me ask one more thing, Mr McCullen. What happened to you in the dream?"

"I was executed by lethal injection – but that makes no sense. There's no death penalty in England."

"There could be in the future," he said. "I had such a dream after discovering the journal. Not the same, of course. I dreamt of my own death. Reading the journal cursed me with recurrent nightmares of my death – just like the curse of the creature in his unpublished story, which is inside the journal. *The Call of the Shakologoth*. In my nightmares, I'm in my study talking when someone hits me over the head with a desk lamp. They beat me to death – but I don't know why. I'm hoping I can stop it happening with your help. Please come to see me. Together, we might prevent the curse from killing us."

"Forget it," I said. "Don't call me again."

I hung up on him. "Lunatic."

I prided myself on being a rational man. I liked reading Lovecraft, but I did not believe in curses and Ancient Gods. My dream had been nothing to do with looking at the journal. It was only a coincidence. I wasn't going to get myself sucked into the madness of Silas Smith.

That night I had the same dream. I woke with the pain of the lethal injection still coursing through my body, knowing I had to stop it from happening again. Very reluctantly, I called Silas Smith again. He picked up his phone on the first ring.

"Another dream?" he said. "Ready to accept the truth now?"

"Okay, Mr Smith. I'm not saying I believe you – but I want to see the journal."

"Come to America," he said. "I'll show you it."

My wife would kill me if she found out what I intended to do – spending our money on a flight to America – so I made up some lies about going to a conference in London, then booked myself a seat on a Virgin Atlantic plane going to New York. I paid for a seat in business class so I could sleep on the journey – but as soon as I closed my eyes and relaxed enough to sleep the same nightmare jolted me awake. Other passengers looked at me like I was a member of Al Qaeda because I must have cried out.

"Are you okay, sir?" A smiling member of the crew asked me.

"Bad dream," I said. "Sorry."

After that, I didn't dare rest. I arrived in New York haggard and weary, shuffling through the airport security too tired to feel anything. I'd booked a rental car which I picked up and drove out of the city, barely remembering to drive on the other side of the road from normal.

Silas Smith's home was in a small coastal town in upstate New York called Slaughterhead. It sounded like the perfect place for a Lovecraftian tale. I started driving there with a clear blue sky overhead – but the weather worsened when I was just a few miles from the town. Black thunderstorms appeared, turning day into night as I was passing a sign for Slaughterhead. The sky unleashed hard rain and slivers of lightning, and a wild wind rocked my car. *Welcome to Slaughterhead* stated another sign blasted by rain. My GPS guided me through the dark streets up a narrow road on the cliffs above the raging Atlantic Ocean. It was impossible to see much through my windscreen as the wipers struggles to sluice away an absolute torrent. There was a Stygian blackness out there. Just like in a Lovecraft story. I could see nothing beyond my car except when lightning lit the road in photo flashes, revealing the nearness of the cliff. I slowed down and had to trust the GPS to show me the way. My destination was Slaughterhead Point, a spit of land sticking out into the ocean like a crooked finger. At its end stood an old lighthouse where Silas Smith lived.

I parked next to a black SUV and ventured out into the freezing rain, thunder rumbling over my head. I was wearing a suit suitable for a change in the weather – but I had not brought a heavy waterproof coat with me. I was soaked to my skin within seconds of leaving my vehicle. As I hurried towards the lighthouse, I looked up at the clouds until I reached the shelter of an alcove next to the main door. I hammered on it until it opened. A surprised woman looked me up and down as I dripped water from my nose. She said something lost in the thunder.

"Hello!" I shouted. "I'm Ian McCullen. I'm looking for Silas Smith."

"My husband's in his study," she said. "I'm Diane. Come in! You'll die of cold out there!"

"Thank you."

It was warm and cosy inside the hall once the door was closed. The thick walls dulled the sounds of the storm. Diane took my wet coat and hung it up. "Silas told me to expect you.

He says you're from England. I expect you are used to bad weather!"

"Not quite like this," I said. "Is it often like this?"

"No," she said. "It's just been like that for a few days. Since my husband returned with *that* journal. It's like it brought the storm with it. I hate that journal Silas is obsessed with it. He hasn't been himself since that awful thing came into our lives."

"Have you read it?"

Diane shuddered. "Me? No. I don't even like to be in the same room as it. It's creepy. It looks like something from hell."

"Just like in a Lovecraft story," I said with a smile.

She grimaced, finding my comment not amusing. "I wouldn't know about Lovecraft. I *never* read horror. I prefer romance and mysteries. I could never understand my husband's obsession with horror. I don't like to be scared when I'm reading. It's not fun." She shivered. "Well, can I get you some coffee or tea? I think we have some Earl Grey."

"I'd love some coffee. Strong and black, please. No sugar."

"My husband's down those stairs in the room on the right. Watch your head on the low doorway. This place wasn't built for tall people."

"It's an unusual home."

"Yes. Silas inherited it from his grandfather. I'd prefer to live in a normal house, but I supposed it has character. I'll get on with making your coffee."

I thanked her again, then I descended a spiral staircase to another door. I knocked as it thundered again. "Mr Smith, it's Ian McCullen."

"It's not locked," he said. "Please come in."

I entered a room cluttered with books. Some libraries didn't have as many books. They were on shelves and stacked on the floor in great towers, nearly touching the ceiling. A sharp, musty odour stung my nostrils. I normally loved the smell of old books because they remind me of my local library, where I first fell in love with literature – but the ones in his study smelled mouldy and unpleasant. Between two bookcases, I could see an oak desk where Silas was sitting in a swivel chair, which he spun around to face me.

"It is so good to see you," he said. "It's an absolute pleasure meeting you in the flesh."

I wished I could say the same to him and mean it, but his sallow appearance shocked me. Silas Smith was a very ill man. His skin was grey, his eyes bloodshot, and his cheeks sunken in shadows, starkly showing the shape of his skull. Though he was not much older than I was, everything about the man looked aged and worn out.

"I haven't slept a wink in two weeks," he said, reading my face. "My death dream haunts me, keeping me awake. I've become a terrible insomniac, but I've worked out how to please the Shakologoth. I have to make other people look at the journal so it can inhabit their dreams. I'm going to send everyone on my email list a copy of the journal. The Shakologoth will reward me with a longer life."

"You'll curse them?"

"I don't have a choice."

He turned to his computer. He was going to click SEND when I grabbed the nearest heavy object, a desk lamp, bludgeoning him with it until he was dead.

Behind me, I heard his wife scream.

She rushed away. I could have chased her. I could have killed her. But that was what the Shakologoth wanted. More death. The death had to stop with mine. I already knew my fate.

I'd seen it in my dreams.

NIGHT HUNT

We must get away this time. We must. Our feet crunch in the snow, leaving a trail that ends at the cabin where we live with the ghosts. My sister pulls her coat around her, shivering, her face flushed with the effort of climbing the wooded hill. Her breath freezes.

"Will they catch us?"

"Not if we keep going," I say, though I am uncertain because the ghosts have chased us before when we've tried to escape. They moved faster than us because they didn't leave imprints in the snow.

The trees whisper around us.

"Come back, come back!"

But we do not listen. There is a light ahead, a glow, a warm place, a living space, away from the ghosts in the cabin – our parents, Martha and Henry, trapped in their eternal damnation caused by their deeds.

I hear my parents' ghosts calling.

"Come back, come back!"

We are almost at the top of the hill when I feel icy fingers on my shoulders, pulling me back.

My sister yells. "No – let her go!"

But they grab her too.

They drag us back, back to the cabin, back to the darkness, back to the bathroom, showing us again why we can't leave, not yet, not ever.

My body is in the bath, cooling in a crimson pool, facing my sister's pale, lifeless corpse, drained of blood by the foolish pact we had made so long ago, thinking we could escape the ghosts by becoming like them, cold and dead.

Author's note: *Some publishers have strict word limits. The magazine I wrote that ghost story for wanted flash stories* under *250 words. This story was 249. The magazine went out of business before I sent it off – which is an all-too-common event, unfortunately – so I thought I'd put it in this collection instead. I added an extra word to make it a nice round number.*

SHELL HOUSE

That strange spring, I rented a small cottage in the Peak District once owned by my family, back when my great-grandfather Sir Thomas Mullford was a wealthy industrialist. His eldest son Daniel had lost our family fortune drinking and gambling before I was born, but I had always wanted to visit the area with my wife, Thea, who loved genealogy and history more than I did. The cottage was on an island in the middle of a tranquil lake surrounded by brooding dark hills. It was the perfect getaway from our busy lives in London. We had not been to the Midlands before.

One morning, my wife and I explored the lake in a rowing boat and discovered the empty shell of a house hidden in the woods on the northern bank. I didn't know that the house had also belonged to my family until I asked my elderly Uncle Stephen about it that evening. He had lived in a houseboat for the last forty years and knew the local history better than any historian. He tapped his pipe on the wooden deck of his houseboat and blew smoke over the water, looking in the direction of the old house, which could be seen in good light as a dark spot on the hillside.

"Back in the 1930s. a young couple like you two lived there. They were called George and Clarissa Mountjoy. They were artists invited by Sir Thomas to stay for the summer. They held some extravagant parties that were the talk of the county. Some people say they indulged in all kinds of depravity with some of the richest people around, like drugs and the occult. I heard they died after a fire started downstairs when they were sleeping. They woke up – but could not get down the stairs. They were forced to go up into the attic, where they burned to death. That house has been left up there ever since because nobody felt right about tearing it down. It is a real shame. It was a beautiful home in its heyday."

"It's not now," I said. "It's not even got a back wall."

"Yes, it does," he said. "You just didn't see it properly. Go back tomorrow morning when it's misty. Then you'll see how beautiful it can look."

"How do you know it will be misty tomorrow?"

"It's always misty in the morning. It's the magic in the air."

Magic? My uncle had been slowly losing his mind for several years – but his earnestness made me go back alone the next morning when the valley was misty. I rowed along the shore until the house came into view high above me, glimpsed through the thick mist. In the morning light, the house did look beautiful – ethereal, ghostly, like something from another time. I thought I saw someone looking out of the attic window – but they vanished as I approached. For a minute I saw the house as it had been – grand and elegant – but the sun burned away the mist, leaving just the blackened shell.

I shook my head and smiled. I had let my uncle's words work on my imagination. I had not really seen the house looking intact. It was only a shell.

I took some photographs and rowed away.

At my desk in our cottage, I uploaded the photographs onto my computer. I studied them closely. I frowned when I saw the last one. The house looked like a ruin – but there was somebody at the attic window. It had not been my imagination. A man or woman was looking down at where I had been taking the photograph – but that was impossible. There were no stairs leading up to the attic. The house had no interior. So, who was it and how had they climbed up there? Zooming in on the window did not improve the fuzziness of the image. The face remained blurred. It was hard to see if the figure was male or female. Too much shadow and darkness surrounded it for a definitive answer.

My wife was asleep – so I sneaked down to the shore and climbed aboard my rowing boat. I rowed it onto the lake and across the silent valley. There was a small jetty under the old ruined house. I rowed towards it and tied my boat to it. Almost invisible, a gravel footpath led up through the woods. I climbed it, smelling the richness of the cool woods and hearing the soft rustle of small animals in the tangled undergrowth. Up and up, winding my way through the mushroom-scented darkness, I climbed until I was high above my boat and the lake. They looked so far away. The woods ended at the house. The house – the shell – was in front of me. I walked gingerly over the rough ground that had once been a path to the entrance, a tall doorway. As I stepped into the shadows, I felt a chill. I stopped about ten feet from the threshold and stared up at the crumbling façade. There was broken glass in some of the windows. The frames had been blackened by the fire. It was incredible the wall stayed upright, creating the illusion of a complete house from the lake.

I removed my camera from my jacket and snapped more pictures. Then I stepped carefully over some nettles and around some giant hogweeds until I was standing on the threshold. I felt a cold breeze on my face and arms. And I felt something else – something on the other side of the doorway, which was in complete darkness. A presence. Watching me. My heart thumped hard against my ribs. There was another person inside the shell of the house.

"Hello?" I said – but nobody answered me.

I was sure I heard whispers and distant music, like a piano playing a tune I could not quite name. Something old. I sensed, rather than saw, two people looking at me. Though I knew it could not be possible. I believed it was George and Clarissa. They wanted me to join them in the dark. They were inviting me in.

As I stared into the gloom, I had the oddest sensation of my life, as though my mind was no longer entirely my own. *Someone was looking through my eyes.* No – two people. I sensed their presence inside me. They wanted me to step into the house and join them in the dark.

It frightened me more than anything.

The darkness was moving closer. It was close to my shoes. In a minute, I feared, it would touch them and I would feel their hands on me, dragging me into the dark.

I backed away and turned and ran down into the woods and down the path. I felt them behind me all the way to my boat. My heart thudding, breathing heavily, I arrived soaked in sweat. I leapt in and sat down, grabbing the oars. I rowed and rowed and never looked back.

Not even once.

666 DOWNING STREET

The PM emerged from Number Ten looking much older and wearier than the robust figure everyone had voted for at the last election. He approached a sea of microphones. "Today I made a deal with the Devil. He will help this great nation out of the worst recession in known history. The Devil is our ally in our time of need. Any questions?"

"Prime Minister, what did you agree to give him?"

"We will have a lottery every week. The winner will be sacrificed live on the BBC News."

"Did you sell your soul, sir?"

"No," he said. "Not mine."

Author's note: *Another 100-word drabble. "A little bit of politics," as Ben Elton used to say when he did stand-up.*

THE JOURNAL

Lena bought the old brownstone believing it had development potential despite its neglected state. The squalid tiny apartments on the second floor had once been homes for Baltimore's poorest citizens – but, if she knocked out some of the plaster walls, she could turn the floor into one large space, which she imagined as a studio perfect for her painting. A friendly contractor told her which walls were load-bearing before she started demolishing the unnecessary ones with a sledgehammer. For days the ancient plaster crumbled under Laura's blows until only one wall remained.

With weary, aching limbs, Lena swung her sledgehammer and made an exploratory hole, exposing another wall of solid bricks just beyond. A cold draught blew out of the hole, smelling musty, tasting like dirt on her tongue. She smashed more plaster away until she could see more of the original wall – then stopped, exhausted.

Lena could see a dusty bookshelf on the second wall. Something lay upon it – something red, covered in stringy cobwebs and dead beetles. It was a velvet cushion with another darker object resting on it. A dusty book. An old one with a leather strap keeping the jacket closed. Strange. Why would anyone leave a book behind a wall?

Lena reached into the gap and grabbed the book. It felt heavy and cold as she pulled it out and examined it in the light.

Nothing identified its contents on the jacket – but it had to be a journal. She blew the dust off it and unhooked the buckle so the pages would open with a soft crackle.

The first page was a dedication: For my love, for my life, here is my tell-tale heart.

Lena noticed the page was signed below. Her own heart thudded when she read the name. Edgar. Lena gasped. Could this journal have belonged to Edgar Allan Poe? Anyone living in Baltimore knew of the city's connection to Poe. He had lived and died there after going insane. Was this book a lost journal? Lena flipped to the next page and read a few poetic sentences written in black ink beside a drawing of a raven.

The Raven was the title of Poe's most famous poem. It could not be a coincidence. Lena shivered. She was holding a valuable historical artefact.

Something fluttered in the corner of her eye. Lena turned and saw a raven perched on the frame of a window she had opened to let in some fresh air. Its black wings fluttered as it settled, its dark, shiny eyes staring at her.

It squawked malevolently, calling out like a screaming banshee.

A second later, another raven joined it.

And another.

And another.

More and more ravens flew through the open windows, blocking out the light, darkening the room, filling the air around Lena with fluttering wings and pecking beaks that drew her blood like a thousand sharp needles.

The ravens stabbed out her eyes – but they did not stop coming.

Blinded, Lena sobbed.

"Nevermore!"

THUDS

Justin and Sarah returned home to Sussex on Sunday morning after spending the week with Sarah's parents. It had been a long week for Justin because his wife's parents were incredibly dull. The first thing Justin did was buy three newspapers from the village shop. Then he walked home and relaxed on the soft leather couch in their living room, while his wife unpacked upstairs. Justin loved reading his Sunday papers in silence, but his peace was disturbed by a hammering from above.

Thud, thud, thud.

It pounded in his head, giving him a throbbing headache, making reading impossible. He tossed his Sunday Times on the living room sofa and stepped out into the hall.

Thud, thud, thud.

The sound was coming down the stairs. Its source was the attic. Each thud shook the lights at the top of the stairs, dropping dust and cobwebs onto the new carpet.

Thud, thud, thud.

More dust. More noise.

Justin sighed.

What was his wife Sarah doing up there? Why couldn't she just relax like him on the weekends?

Sarah was always trying to fix up their home so they could put it on the market and sell it for a decent profit. She was always complaining about their house being a pigsty, which was a serious exaggeration.

Their house had been built in the 1940s and had belonged to his parents. It had six bedrooms and a large garden at the back, where Justin grew tomatoes just like his dad did. The house was old – but Justin grew up loving it. He had dreamt of having a family living there. After his parents died, Justin had persuaded Sarah to move out of their tiny rented flat in London to the suburbs of Essex. The house was in the beautiful little village where he had been born. For the last two years, Sarah had hated living there because she liked living in the city. Chief among her complaints was the general state of the house, which had not been redecorated since the late 1970s. They had spent thousands decorating the downstairs, then the bedrooms, leaving only the attic in its original condition. His parents had only used the attic for storage. That seemed a sensible thing to Justin. You needed a space for all the crap you didn't want to throw away. He didn't see the point of spending time and money changing it. It wasn't like they wanted to live up there.

Thud, thud, thud.

Justin climbed the stairs and stopped at the bottom of the loft ladder, looking up into the darkness.

"Sarah, what are you doing?"

Thud, thud, thud.

The noise was really getting on his nerves.

"Sarah, what are you doing?"

Justin didn't want to go up the ladder wearing his slippers – but his wife was still hammering away, probably wearing her earphones so she didn't have to listen to the noise she was creating. He would have to go up to tell her to stop. Or at least keep the noise down a bit. She didn't have to hammer so hard that the ceiling shook. What was she hammering, anyway?

Thud, thud, thud.

The attic was the only room Justin had never liked. In truth, he was a little afraid of it. There was no electricity up there except for a cable hanging from a rafter with a 40-watt bulb attached. That bulb never provided much light in the big space under the eaves. Very reluctantly, Justin grabbed the ladder and set his right foot on the bottom rung. The ladder creaked under his weight as he climbed up it and poked his head through the trapdoor opening into the gloom.

In his childhood, Justin had been terrified of going up there in the dark and cold. He had imagined all kinds of monsters lurking in the darkness – ghosts, vampires, zombies, cannibalistic mutants – but he had got over that fear when he was an adult. At least he thought he had. Now he smelled the mustiness and felt a chill that reminded him of his childhood fears.

Thud, thud, thud.

The single bulb cast a very weak light. He could barely see the shapes of the storage boxes and old furniture. Most of the attic was in solid blackness.

THUD, THUD, THUD.

The hammering was much louder now – but he could not see his wife in the bulb's light. Was she hammering away in the dark at the far side? He could not see beyond a solid oak beam supporting the roof. The light did not reach beyond it. He walked towards it calling her name.

THUD, THUD, THUD.

On the other side of the beam, Justin's eyes started adjusting to the low light level. There – in the semi-darkness - he could see his wife sitting on the floor, facing him. Her long red hair hid her face. She was wearing one of his old shirts and a pair of cut-off jeans that she only wore when she was doing DIY. She called them her Daisy Dukes. Justin thought she looked really sexy in them – normally. Not that day. No. Something was horribly wrong with what he was seeing.

There was a box of one hundred six-inch nails between her bare legs. A glistening claw hammer was in her right hand, rising and falling, smashing down with all of her strength.

THUD! THUD! THUD!

Justin could not believe what his wife was doing to herself. She was *hammering* the nails into her legs, giving each nail three quick hard blows until it penetrated through her flesh and bone into the wood beneath.

He felt sick.

Her legs were nailed to the floorboards, blood running from dozens of puncture wounds. Her blood was pooling under her. There were dozens of nails in each leg, from her feet to her upper thighs.

She must have had some kind of mental breakdown to self-harm like that. It was the only explanation Justin could think of as he rushed towards her, grasping for the hammer. She didn't want to let go and fought him for it. Justin struggled to prise her fingers off it.

"Stop it, Sarah. Stop it. You're hurting yourself." Justin yanked the hammer from her hand. It was warm and wet. Blood dripped down it onto the floorboards. Disgusted, Justin tossed it into the dark, where it landed somewhere with a crash, breaking something. Then he inspected Sarah's self-inflicted injuries. There were over thirty nails in her feet and legs. They were firmly pinning her to the floor. Her hot blood covered her skin in a red sheen. It was oozing out of her wounds like stigmata. "God! You need an ambulance. You're bleeding all over."

Justin wished he had his phone – but it was downstairs in its charger. Where was Sarah's? It was too dark to see if his wife had hers. It was possibly in the back pocket of her Daisy Dukes.

"Oh, baby, what have you done?"

Sarah answered with a horrible, frightening mewling cry that sounded like a kitten in extreme agony. Justin noticed something else as he looked at her face. The shiny flat head of a nail was sticking out of her lower jaw. And there were other nail heads protruding from above her upper lip, like studs. Some of those nails had gone through her lower jaw to poke out as sharp points under her chin.

Justin moaned. His wife had nailed her mouth completely closed. She had to be in complete agony.

Why would she do that to herself?

How could she do that?

The pain had to be so intense that a normal person would have passed out after the first nail went in.

"Sarah, listen to me. I want to call for help. Do you have your phone?"

In her current mental state Justin did not expect her to answer him, but she shook her head. No.

"Okay. I will have to go downstairs. I'll come straight back once I've called for an ambulance."

Sarah mewled again. Tears ran down her cheeks. She shook her head violently.

"You don't want me to do that?"

She groaned. Then she mumbled something. The strain of trying to speak with her mouth nailed shut caused blood to pour from her lips and run down her chin and chest. Her fingers clawed at the nails in her jaw. She was trying to remove them *so she could tell him something*.

"No! Don't pull at them," he said. "You'll do more damage taking them out."

Justin didn't know what to do. He could not leave her alone. She could hurt herself even more. Pulling the nails out was worse than leaving them in. He grabbed her hands and stopped her. They were face to face. He saw fear in her eyes. She mumbled again, her eyes pleading him to understand her words. Justin listened hard as she struggled to speak without opening her mouth. She wasn't easy to understand. It was like listening to a bad ventriloquist speaking with a mouthful of water, only it was hot blood filling her throat. Justin realised what she was struggling to say. Bit by bit, she communicated what had happened.

Two hours earlier Sarah had come up to the attic to repair a loose floorboard — but there had been a man hiding up there. The man attacked her, knocking her out. She woke up in pain with the man standing behind her, hammering nails into her face. The man then nailed her feet to the floor so she could not escape. After that, he gave her the hammer, instructing her to use it on herself. He ordered her to nail her legs to the floor, not stopping until she had used them all. He told her to nail herself all the way up to her hips. He told her to not stop until she had used all the nails. He warned her that he'd kill Justin if she did not use the entire box of nails. If she failed to use every nail, the man had promised to kill Justin in front of her and then kill her with the remaining nails. The only way to save her own life and Justin's was to follow the man's sick instructions. Nailing herself to the floor.

As Justin listened to her crazy story, he wondered if his lovely wife was telling the truth or delusional. It was hard to believe a strange man had been hiding in their attic. But it was harder to believe his wife would willingly nail herself to the floor. He wanted to believe her.

"What man?" Justin said. "What man forced you to do this?"

"Me," someone said behind him.

Justin spun around just as a torch flicked on, blinding him with its intensity. Somewhere beyond the torchlight, the man was standing. Justin's instinct was to run at the man who had tortured Sarah – but he could not even see him. The light shone in his eyes until the man lowered it to show him a long hunting knife. The wicked blade gleamed in the beam.

"Try anything and I'll gut you," the man beyond the light said. His voice was cold and deep.

"What do you want?"

"I want you to finish what your wife started. Take the rest of the nails and hammer them into your wife's legs. They must go all the way through – so hit them hard. I'll let you both live if you do it, Justin. Nail her."

"No. I'm not doing that. I can't."

"Do it or I'll kill her," the man said. "And then I'll use the spare nails on you."

Justin shook his head. "Please don't make me do that." He

thought of an excuse. "I don't have the hammer. I can't do it without the hammer."

"Yes, I saw you throw it away. Here. Have it back."

The hammer landed at his feet. Justin stared at the blood on it. He didn't want to touch it.

The man sighed. "Your wife is bleeding to death, Justin. The faster you do it, the more chance she has of surviving. Pick it up and use it, Justin. Hammer the nails like a good little boy."

Justin picked it up. It was a heavy weapon. A good weapon to use on the man. He imagined smashing it into the man's skull with a satisfying thunk. His hand tightened around it.

The man chuckled. "I know what you're thinking, Justin. You're wondering if you could kill me. But I doubt a man like you knows how to fight. You're overweight and unfit. You're slow, Justin. Too slow. I'm half your age and very fit, Justin. I'm also very fast. And I don't play fair. You'd only get one chance against my knife. So ... if you want to go for it, I'm waiting."

Justin did not move.

The man sighed. "Jeez, Justin! Make your mind up. Sarah's dying. Make a decision. Attack me or use the nails on your wife."

His wife was looking at him and nodding miserably. She *wanted* him to do what the man said. It was the only way to survive – but it was not right. There had to be something he could do. Maybe if he started doing what the man said, he could get an opportunity to attack when the maniac was off his guard?

"Okay, okay," he said. "I'll do it."

Justin was sobbing when he grabbed the first nail. There were about forty left in the box. Forty times he would hurt his wife. With the maniac shining a light on him, Justin's hand trembled as he placed it against his wife's left leg, hoping he would not slice an artery when he hammered it in. I'm so sorry, he thought, raising the hammer.

THUD THUD THUD.

The nail went through her leg into the board.

He grabbed another. He hammered it in. Sarah sobbed. She writhed in pain. Justin speeded up. THUD THUD THUD. His own bloody fingers struggled to hold the next nail. THUD THUD THUD. Sarah moaned and moaned. Justin worked as fast as he could, hating himself, hating the man, hating the world. He continued until the box was almost empty. There were just two left when the man spoke again.

"I don't want you coming after me, Justin. Use the last two to nail your own feet to the floor."

The new request wasn't as bad as using them on his wife. Justin put the penultimate nail on his foot and banged it in. THUD THUD THUD. The pain made him groan. He did the same thing with the last nail.

"There! It's done! Now, will you please go?"

The man did not reply. He was backing away, keeping the torch shining in Justin's eyes until he was on the ladder. Then the man was escaping. Justin heard him padding down the stairs and a distant door slamming.

The man had gone.

Justin was afraid it was a trick.

He expected the man to come back.

The house was silent.

Justin's feet pulsed with pain.

Sarah was no longer making any noise. She was unconscious. Her breathing was raspy. It sounded like she was choking on her own blood.

Justin pried the nails out of his own feet, screaming at the pain. Standing unsteadily, he turned his wife's head so she stopped swallowing blood, then he hobbled to the trapdoor. He looked back at his wife and made a promise. "I'll come back. Just don't die. Stay alive, baby. I'll save you."

Light-headed from his own loss of blood, Justin climbed down the ladder, feeling fresh pain with each foot placed down on the rungs.

His socks and shoes felt like they were twice as heavy, now that they were soaked in his cooling blood.

Back on the landing, Justin could no longer stand up. The pain was too much. He crawled on his hands and knees to the top of the stairs. He descended them by sliding down them on his bottom, keeping his feet well off the ground.

There was no sign of the man downstairs when he crawled into the living room. He was relieved – but wary.

His phone was still in its charger. It was fully charged now. Justin wiped his bloodstained hands on the carpet before grabbing it and making a frantic 999 call, hoping the authorities would send an ambulance for his wife before she died.

*

Four months later, Justin pushed Sarah's wheelchair into their new home, a ground-floor flat in central London. Sarah looked pale and gaunt after her long hospital stay. She had lost her legs and still needed some operations to fix her mouth – but she was alive and getting better, slowly. Her recovery was still incomplete – but she looked happy to be out in the real world. Justin showed her around the rooms. The whole flat had been designed to be wheelchair accessible.

"Do you like it?"

Sarah could not yet speak again. She had endured painful surgery to repair her palate, tongue and jaw. Her mouth was in a hideous contraption of wires and metal plates, making speech impossible. She wrote her answer on a tablet and showed him the screen.

It's great. Very modern.

"Yeah, I thought you'd want a change from my old house. I'm glad you like it. Check out the view."

He pushed her to the window. There was a stunning view across the Thames.

Sarah wrote something else.

It's lovely, but I'm v tired. I'd like to go to bed.

"Oh, right," Justin said. He wheeled her into the bedroom, where he carefully lifted her out of the wheelchair and carried her to the bed. She weighed next to nothing in his arms. Not without her legs. The doctors could not save them because of the vascular damage. There were bandages over her stumps, which she had covered with her skirt. He helped her undress and change into her nightgown. Justin could not look at her body without thinking of the nails and what he had been forced to do. She had lost her legs because of him, because of his cowardice. He should have fought the man. Maybe then his wife would not be disabled. Maybe then he could feel like had not let her down.

Sarah was taking so many drugs for her pain that she was asleep in a minute. He kissed her tousled red hair and slipped out of the room, blinking tears. He thought about the attack again. It seemed like only yesterday. He found it hard to believe fourth months had passed. It was harder to believe the police had caught nobody.

For a time – while Sarah was in a medically-induced coma – the police had suspected him of attempted murder because they had found DNA or any other physical evidence to prove another man had been there, coercing him to hurt Sarah. They suspected Justin had injured himself only to give credence to his story. They did not believe his version until Sarah woke up and confirmed it. By then, it was too late. The real criminal had got away with the crime.

Since that terrible day, Justin had become obsessed with catching the man himself. He turned on his computer and clicked on one of the many websites he had bookmarked during his own investigation. There was no new information.

That afternoon, Sarah was awake again. She relaxed on their couch using her tablet to talk to him.

Justin, I've been thinking about HIM a lot.

"What about him?"

He didn't know I was going to go up into the attic. So, what was he doing up there before I interrupted him?

"I don't know."

There was nothing of value?

"No. Just my parents' old stuff. Junk."

There must have been something.

"No. There was nothing. I cleared it all out before selling the place. There really was nothing of any value. I swear it."

Then there must have been another reason.

"I agree – but what?"

What else was in the attic?

"Um. The cold water tank. Electrical cables. Gas pipes."

Gas pipes?

"Yeah. They supply the hot water tank. They run under the floorboards."

Sarah typed frantically.

That's it! He was intending to mess with the gas. He wanted to kill us in a gas explosion, but I ruined his plan. Attacking me was never part of his plan. The maniac improvised to cover up what he was really doing.

"Which was what?"

I don't know yet. But I will.

Justin saw the determined look on his wife's face and realised he was not the only one obsessed with finding their attacker. Together, they would find him and make him pay for what he had done.

It took another week before Sarah showed him the results of her marathon sessions of web surfing.

Justin, I found something interesting about a company called Woolrich Holdings. In the last four years, they've been buying dozens of houses damaged in gas explosions. All the houses bought are in the same area as ours. The company buys the properties for next to nothing and builds new homes, making a tidy profit, according to their company report. Woolrich Holdings is solely owned by a man called Anthony

Woolrich. He's personally made millions. Just look at the pictures of his own home on his website. It's a massive mansion.

Justin looked at the pictures of Anthony Woolrich's huge home, which had acres of woodland surrounding it, including a tennis court and stables for his thoroughbred horses. "Sarah, I don't see the connection. Woolrich Holdings didn't buy our home."

No – but I believe they would have if it had been destroyed in a gas explosion.

"You don't have any proof, Sarah."

I know that - but it is a possibility. You'll have to check out the company for me. I have to know if Woolrich was the man in our attic.

Justin knew the evidence against Woolrich was thin, non-existent really, just a hunch of his wife's. But since he had nothing else to go on, he would do it. He would investigate.

Justin started the next day by visiting a wi-fi café where he could do some research with no links left behind for the police to follow. He found out more about Anthony Woolrich's business and personal life from Facebook and LinkedIn.

Woolrich had been married twice – first when he was twenty, then when he was fifty-nine. His second wife was a Polish model half his age called Izabela. They had three pretty daughters in private schools. Woolrich loved posting pictures of himself at fund-raising events and humble-bragging about giving generous donations to charities. He also took many selfies playing tennis, golf and yachting.

Justin could find nothing indicating the man was capable of committing evil violence. He had no criminal record, but he had points on his driver's licence for speeding.

That was all.

It disappointed Justin. There was no smoking gun. Even Woolrich's business looked completely legitimate. It had existed for eight years without any legal issues. Justin wondered what Woolrich had done before that. There was nothing on his LinkedIn profile about his previous jobs and businesses. That seemed a little odd, like he had white-washed his past. Justin decided to go back further, using the government's records. He learnt Woolrich Holdings was not Anthony Woolrich's first business. His first one had gone into administration in 1992 owing several hundred customers thousands of pounds each. His second one had also failed. Many investors had lost a lot of money – but Woolrich had protected his own assets by keeping his house and cars solely in his wife's name. It looked like millions of pounds had disappeared from his dodgy businesses into his own pockets, though there was no proof. Looking deeper, Justin discovered the police had investigated Woolrich for fraud in 1994 and again in 1998, though no charges had been brought. The investigations had been dropped due to a lack of evidence.

"His unethical business practices are not a smoking gun," Justin said when he returned home to Sarah. "But I think the gun's definitely got a warm barrel. He's not as nice as he wants people to believe. He could be the man we're looking for. The big question is, what do you want me to do next?"

Sarah was in her wheelchair looking out at the grey water of the Thames. She typed her reply. It was all in capital letters as though she was shouting.

MAKE HIM TELL THE TRUTH.

"How?"

ABDUCT HIM AND INTERROGATE HIM.

"Abduct him? That's a big step, baby. What if we're wrong about him? What if he's innocent? I'd be breaking the law and harming an innocent man."

Do you think he is?

"No," Justin said.

Then do it. Do it for me. FIND OUT THE TRUTH.

"Okay."

Thank you for doing this, Justin. I love you.

Justin worked out what he would do the next day. An abduction required meticulous planning. He was aided by Izabella's Twitter messages, which revealed she was excited about taking her children on a weekend shopping spree to New York. Her husband was staying alone in England for two days. It was the perfect opportunity to get Woolrich alone. Justin drove down the country on Wednesday and observed Woolrich's home from a long distance through digital binoculars. He observed security cameras at the gates and on the walls around the estate. It was likely more cameras covered the mansion and grounds, making it a poor location for abducting Woolrich.

Justin picked another place, somewhere with less surveillance. He knew enough about Woolrich's life to scout out the golf course where he played regularly on Saturday mornings. The parking area near the clubhouse only had one camera. It did not cover the whole car park – just the entrance to the building. Visitors parked around the side where a sign warned drivers they parked at their own risk. There were no cameras. That was good. Even better, there was dense shrubbery close to the parking spaces.

On Saturday morning, Justin parked a rented white van close to the golf course. He had covered the interior with plastic sheeting to keep it clean when he returned it. He had also brought along everything he needed to blindfold, gag and secure his prisoner. He was nervous – but determined. With a self-made cosh hidden in his dark coat, he left the van. It was a warm and sunny day, the ideal day for having a leisurely stroll, not for an abduction. He felt strange as he walked towards the golf course with his mind racing, rehearsing what he was going to do. There was still time to change his mind. He had done nothing illegal yet. He could forget it and go home. No – that was a lie. His home was gone forever. The man in the attic had violated it. Justin had to know if Anthony Woolrich was that man. Justin sneaked behind the clubhouse through the woods. He slipped into the shrubbery and waited for Woolrich.

Woolrich arrived alone at nine in a black Land Rover. He was talking on his smartphone when he walked around to the back of his vehicle, opening the back with a beep-beep of his electronic key. Justin watched him remove his clubs. For a moment, Woolrich had his back to Justin. Justin would have made his move then if there had been nobody around – but other golfers had arrived at the same time. He couldn't have a dozen witnesses. He did nothing. He let Woolrich close his car and go into the clubhouse. Sighing, Justin settled down for a long wait, flicking crawling things off his face, hoping nobody would notice him lying under the bushes.

In the mid-afternoon, Woolrich reappeared in an ebullient mood, laughing and joking with another player. Justin feared he would lose his chance if Woolrich got in his vehicle first, but the other man's blue sports car was closest. The men said goodbye and the other player drove away, leaving Woolrich on his own. Justin inched forward, readying himself. The cosh in his hands felt very heavy. Woolrich was putting his clubs into his car when Justin rushed up behind him and struck him over the head. Woolrich went down on his knees, stunned. Justin hit him again. That was enough to knock out Woolrich. His heart thumping, Justin bundled Woolrich's unconscious body into the back of his own car, stole the keys off the ground, then slammed down the hatch, locking Woolrich in the vehicle. Thirty seconds later, Justin drove away the Land Rover, heading straight for his van.

Woolrich was still knocked unconscious when Justin transferred him into the van. Justin tied him up with rope and tape as a precaution. He also slipped a black hessian bag over the man's head before leaving him in the back. Justin searched him thoroughly, taking his smartphone, wallet and keys. He turned on the smartphone – but it was locked. Next, he went back to the Land Rover and searched it. He found another phone in the glove compartment. It was a basic model – a cheap pay-as-you-go phone with none of the features of Woolrich's expensive smartphone. Why did Woolrich have a second phone? Was it just for emergencies? Or was it for another darker reason? It was also locked. Justin's head pounded. Why was nothing simple?

Though he had been wearing gloves the whole time, Justin cleaned the inside of the Land Rover before abandoning it.

He drove to an old farmhouse that had been derelict for many years. He had already set up an interrogation room with a chair bolted to the floor. He put Woolrich on it and tied him down. He put on a biker's helmet to hide his face before removing the hessian bag. Woolrich looked unconscious – but Justin suspected him of faking it. Justin used smelling salts to jerk him awake. He stepped back as the man opened his eyes and saw him standing with a hammer in one hand and a phone in the other.

"Uurgh. What's going on? Who are you? Why've you kidnapped me?"

Hearing Woolrich's panicky voice, Justin knew straight away he wasn't the man in the attic. The man in the attic had a deeper, throatier voice. It worried Justin. Had he got it all wrong?

"Don't hurt me," the businessman said. "I have three daughters. Please let me go. I can get you some money if that's what you want. You can use my credit cards. I'll give you the PIN codes."

"I don't want money," Justin said. "I want the code to your phone."

"Uh – okay, okay! It's 64217."

Justin typed it into the pay-as-you-go phone.

INVALID PASSWORD.

"That's not right."

"Yes, it is. For my smartphone."

"I want the code for this one."

"That old one? I can't remember the code. It's years since I used it. I only keep it for emergencies in case my car breaks down and I can't use my normal one. Why do you want to know that, anyway? What's this about?"

Woolrich's explanation sounded convincing – but why would he have an emergency phone if he couldn't remember the code?

"I'm giving you one minute to give me the right code," Justin said. "If you don't give me it, I'll put a nail in your right foot."

"I don't know the code! Please! Don't do this! I don't understand why you're doing this to me!"

"Thirty seconds."

"I really can't remember."

"Fifteen seconds."

"I don't know it!"

"Ten seconds."

Justin didn't know what he was going to do when the time ran out. He had hoped the threat alone would make Woolrich tell him – but what if he genuinely could not remember?

"Five. Four. Three. Two. One."

"I don't remember!"

Justin showed Woolrich a nail. The man's eyes widened as he placed it on his bare foot near his toes.

"This will hurt," Justin said, raising the hammer.

"Please! I don't know it!"

THUD THUD THUD.

Woolrich screamed.

Justin produced another nail. "You have another minute to tell me, or I'll nail your other foot."

"Stop. I don't remember."

"Try," Justin said. He counted down. Woolrich begged him to hurt him. The time ran out. Justin saw the fear in the man's eyes as he lifted the hammer up. "Okay then. Here we go again."

"Wait!"

"You remember?"

"Yes."

"Tell me."

"19644."

"Are you sure?"

Woolrich nodded. "Yes."

The number unlocked the handset. Justin looked through the call list and found only one number listed thirty times. He read the texts sent to it. Each contained nothing except a postcode and a house number. One belonged to Justin's home.

"This is my address. You sent it to a man who came to destroy it by tampering with the gas. My wife interrupted him and he made me hammer nails into her legs."

"I know! I'm so sorry! I'm very sorry about your wife. That was not meant to happen. You were not meant to be there when he broke in. He was supposed to cause an accident when nobody was there."

"What's his name?"

"Eddie. Eddie Miller."

"Tell me about him."

"Eddie used to go work for me as a gas fitter. He was good at the job – but he was always a bit of a psycho. He lost his temper around people and freaked out my clients with his weird sense of humour, losing me business. He didn't get on with my other employees. I was afraid of firing him – so I figured out a way of making money burning down houses. I will admit I paid him to make accidents. I put in low bids for the destroyed properties – but I never ever wanted anyone hurt. He's the psycho, not me."

"People died in gas explosions," Justin said. "And my wife lost her legs to that nutter."

"I'm sorry. If you let me go, I promise I won't say a word about what you've done to me. I'll even get you some money. I can pay for your wife's care for the rest of her life. Anything. Just don't kill me. I promise I'll never do it again."

"If you'd felt bad about what he did to my wife, you would have stopped causing accidents. There were two more addresses texted to him after mine. You were quite happy to go on dealing with him – as long as you didn't get caught. There's only one way to save yourself. I want to know everything you know about him right now."

"Then you'll let me live?"

"Yes," Justin said. "I swear I won't kill you."

The next day, Justin sent a text message from Woolrich's phone, providing Eddie the gas fitter with the address of his next job. The address was the home of Sarah's parents. Sarah had persuaded them to visit her in London for the day, leaving the house apparently empty. That morning, Justin waited inside until he heard a soft click from the kitchen door, the sound of Eddie picking the lock. Justin was hiding behind a door when Eddie blithely walked past, carrying a toolbox. Justin cold-cocked him with his cosh. While the man was unconscious, Justin dragged him through the house into the garage, where he had parked his car.

Justin took the gas fitter to where he had left Woolrich alive. Woolrich was still where he had left him lying on the floor.

Justin looked down at the gas fitter, studying him. Eddie looked so ordinary. There was nothing remarkable about him.

Nobody would have noticed him in a crowd. Eddie stripped him naked and strapped his wrists and ankles into leather straps attached to bolts in the floor.

Justin walked outside and phoned Sarah. "I'm coming home. It's all ready for tonight."

It was dark when Eddie awoke.

Justin silently watched him from a shadowy corner of the room as the gas fitter tried to sit up. The restraints stopped him.

"Hey! What's this?" The gas fitter turned his head and saw the other man on the floor. "Tony? Is that you, mate? Jeez!"

Woolrich moaned in reply. It was impossible for him to speak. Six-inch nails were sticking out of his entire body, including his eyes, which had been penetrated into their sockets. Justin had blinded him, but he had left one of his ears intact so he could hear his own screams. Somehow, despite the injuries, despite the pain, Woolrich was still alive and breathing, just like Justin had promised. Woolrich's hundred wounds wept blood onto the floor. Justin pushed Sarah's wheelchair into the light so Eddie could see them both watching him.

"You?" he said. "I should have killed you."

"Too late for regrets," Justin said. "I've brought something for you, Eddie. Look." He showed the gas fitter a hammer and a large box containing a thousand nails. "I'm glad you're awake, Eddie. Let's get started. We are going to be here for a very, very, very long time."

EVE

Growing up around the time they released The Blair Witch Project, my friends and I often talked about the crazy woman living in the woods. Everyone knew she was a witch without ever saying the actual word. She wore black and never spoke to anyone – but she was always watching us whenever we dared go there.

When I was around ten, I discovered one of her grisly altars north of the Wilder's Creek. It consisted of dozens of skulls on spikes, displayed like a macabre piece of art. I was so scared I wet my bed that night and told my foster parents what I'd seen. They phoned the police.

The sheriff at first assumed he was dealing with a serial killer – but forensic tests revealed the skulls were decades old. The sheriff decided it was a sick prank because the skulls had been stolen from a local graveyard.

He arrested a disturbed woman called Eve.

Eve was charged with forty counts of desecration – but she didn't go to jail. She was committed to an asylum, the one on the hill near where I lived. They released her a couple of years later.

The next day, a skull was left outside my window, hanging from a tree branch.

The sheriff looked for Eve – but she had disappeared.

"I don't think she's dangerous, son – but if you see her

again, tell you foster parents to call me."

A few days later, I caught Eve watching me from inside the woods when I was on my way to school. I felt her dark eyes upon me, and I felt my heart thumping. I ran all the way to the gates – but I told nobody. I was too scared.

The next day, she appeared again. I was prepared to run – but I called out instead. "Why are you following me?"

She did not answer.

I moved closer. "What do you want?"

"I'm your real mother," she said. "They stole you from me when you were a baby. They said I was mad – but I am not. I have powers – but they never understood. Come with me. Let me show you."

She stretched out her bony white hand, beckoning me to go with her into the woods. I knew she was sick and crazy and not my real mother – I had been told her name was Karen and she had died giving birth – but a part of me wanted to go with her into the dark. I hated my foster parents, who had only adopted me for the money from the government. What if they had lied? What if she really was my mother?

I stepped towards her.

She took my hand.

We walked deep into the woods to another altar made of skulls.

She stroked my hair, her fingers feeling my head.

"This will be beautiful in my collection."

Luckily, three amateur movie-makers stumbled upon the scene.

I got away while she was killing them.

INTERVIEW WITH A ZOMBIE

INTERVIEWER: Good morning, listeners! I'm honoured to be interviewing Gene Eric Zombie. You won't know his name – but you will recognise him from his uncredited roles in thousands of horror movies playing such diverse roles as Zombie #1 and Zombie #2.

Gene Eric Zombie can be considered the oldest zombie on the block because he was born and died over 2500 years ago in Ancient Egypt, where he was mummified inside a tomb until an archaeological team dug him up. They shipped him to Chicago, where his sarcophagus opened in 1922. Wearing heavy bandages, Gene Eric Zombie returned to life as a reanimated corpse, the first of his kind.

Very hungry, Gene found himself lost in a strange new world, cursed with a second life that compelled him to eat human flesh. He ate several archaeology students and infected dozens of people with his curse, creating an outbreak that resulted in a brief apocalypse. It was a tough time for Gene. His brain-eating addiction forced him to flee the authorities until he found a safe haven in Hollywood among the blood-sucking vampires running the movie business.

Penniless and starving, with no useful skills, Gene had no choice but to become an actor. His early roles in silent movies cast him as a mummy, where his vocal talent for moaning and groaning could not be appreciated. His career would have ended if talkies had not arrived, allowing him to say his first line: "Grrrr!"

That line was an instant hit with audiences. Since that pivotal moment, Gene Eric Zombie has never been out of work. Afraid of being typecast as a mummy, Gene bravely shed his bandages to take on other meatier parts as a cannibalistic killer and lover of fresh human brains. His acting credits include *I'm A Zombie: Let Me Eat a Celebrity*, *Dead or Not Dead* and *Catching Up With The Kardashians,* a reality show that ended abruptly after two episodes once Gene caught up with them.

Thanks for doing this interview, Gene.

GENE ERIC ZOMBIE: Grrrr!

INTERVIEWER: Excuse the chains tying you to your chair, but I've heard you have a reputation on set for biting people. Is that rumour true?

GENE ERIC ZOMBIE: Grrrr!

INTERVIEWER: Don't want to answer, huh? Okay. I'll ask something else. Fans love your movies for their gruesome realism, which is created by you actually biting and killing people. Which actor did you most like eating?

GENE ERIC ZOMBIE: Grrrr!

INTERVIEWER: I'm not familiar with that actor. Hope he tasted good! I imagine you get asked this next one all the time – but I'll ask it, anyway. What's your favourite movie?

GENE ERIC ZOMBIE: Grrrr!

INTERVIEWER: Uh. Okay. Let's move on. It says in my notes that you had to deal with a lot of prejudice in the 1940s and 1950s. You were brought in front of the House of Undead-

American Activities where you made a powerful speech that changed many people's ideas about the living dead. Your speech changed attitudes to the zombie community. How does that feel?

GENE ERIC ZOMBIE: Grrrr!

INTERVIEWER: Groups of vigilantes used to hunt the living dead down and shoot them in the head, even if they had committed no crimes. You had no rights and couldn't vote. It must have been hard starting your career as an undead actor, facing such prejudice?

GENE ERIC ZOMBIE: Grrrr!

INTERVIEWER: Yes, it would make me angry, too. You had a small role in *Night of the Living Dead* directed by George Romero. Was he an easy director to work with?

GENE ERIC ZOMBIE: Grrrr!

INTERVIEWER: Hmm. I must say you're not being very cooperative. Are the chains too tight?

GENE ERIC ZOMBIE: Grrrr!

INTERVIEWER: I'll just loosen them a little. There.

GENE ERIC ZOMBIE: Grrrr!

INTERVIEWER: Hey! Don't bite me! Ow! That hurts! Don't eat my brain!

GENE ERIC ZOMBIE: Grrrr!

INTERVIEWER: Grrrr!

GENE ERIC ZOMBIE: Grrrr!

The interview ended at that point with several untimely deaths.

Publicly humiliated, Gene Eric Zombie moved to England and entered politics.

Today, he can often be heard in the House of Commons, moaning incoherently on the back benches, where he is among his peers.

THE FLASH

On the few hot days of the British summer, I loved sleeping with a window open to let in a cool breeze – but I often suffered from allergies as a result. To reduce my symptoms, I always swallowed a pre-emptive allergy tablet before going to bed. It usually worked wonders. But one morning the council started cutting the grass at an unholy hour, unleashing an invisible cloud of pollen and grass allergens into the air that my immune system could not cope with.

I woke with my head feeling like it was clogged with wet concrete, my eyes and nose streaming as I lumbered out of bed, quickly heading for the open window. The smell of freshly mown grass was sweet and cloying. Sneezing so hard my brain rattled, I heard a deep humming noise outside, which turned out to be the sound of two big red grass-cutting machines on the verge opposite our house. It was only seven – but the grass-cutting machines were already trimming the grass on the other side of the road. Both drivers wore protective masks as they zoomed around like Formula One racers. They were lucky. They didn't have to breathe in the nasty stuff they were releasing into the air. I hated them. Did they have to cut the grass so early?

I slammed the window shut and considered going back to bed – but I needed an anti-histamine first. Of course, there were none left in the packet by the bed. That meant I had to go to the bathroom to search the medicine cabinet. No – none there either.

It was a *great* start to my day.

Feeling like I'd been sucker-punched, I went down the stairs to the kitchen, where Laura was feeding our kids their breakfast while watching the news on the TV. Sam and Rachel, our eight-year-old twins, were scooping cereal into their mouths like they'd never been fed before. They were wearing their very expensive school uniforms that I hoped would remain stain-free. They didn't even notice me in the room because they were pulling faces at each other.

I looked at the TV through blurry eyes. The main story was the heatwave affecting Britain. A meteorologist was saying it was connected to some unusual sunspot activity. The sun was going through an active phase, resulting in higher levels of radiation striking the upper atmosphere, causing dramatic light shows. Strange unpredictable weather was happening as the sun baked the country. The meteorologist sounded like a doom-sayer, though the interviewer assured viewers it was not dangerous because the atmosphere stopped the radiation.

"Lauba, dub yub hab ebby anti-hista-bins?"

My family all turned to face me, looking surprised to see me up. They didn't see me get up this early under normal circumstances – not after I'd lost my job last month. I'd turned into a sloth without a good reason for getting up in the morning.

"What's that, Phil?" Laura said. "I can't understand a word you're saying."

That was because my nose was blocked up. I blew it and repeated my words slowly, making each word a little clearer. "I said, 'Do you have any anti-histamines?'"

"Oh! Try the kitchen drawer," Laura suggested. "Think there's an old pack in there."

"Which drawer? This one?" I just saw knives and forks and

spoons.

"No – the other one. No – not that one. The *other* other one."

Ah! I found some anti-histamines behind some batteries at the back of the drawer. They were seriously out of date – but they'd work. I swallowed one with some water, then slumped at the kitchen table, blowing my nose into tissue after tissue.

"Dad, you look terrible," Sam said. "Are you turning into a zombie?"

"I wish," I said. "No. It's my grass allergy. Those idiots from the council cut the grass again. It sets me off every time. You kids are lucky you don't get it. I feel like I've caught Ebola."

"What's that?" Sam said.

Laura glared at me. She didn't want me scaring them. "Nothing," I said. "Finish your breakfast, Sam."

Sam was nearly finished with his cereal when his sister pulled a face that made him laugh, spilling milk and soggy Coco Pops on his shirt. Rachel giggled as her brother stood up, dripping chocolate milk onto the floor. The front of his shirt and trousers were soaked in a brown mess. "Mum, I'm all wet, but it's Rachel's fault. She made me laugh!"

My wife swore to herself. "You'll have to change – but I don't have time to wait. I've got an important meeting. Phil, you'll have to take the kids to school. Can you do that?"

I had nothing else to do. "Yeah, sure. You go. I'll get them to school."

"You can handle that, right?"

I sighed. Since I'd lost my job, Laura treated me like I was another kid, not her husband. "I know how to get them to school, Laura. I'm not completely useless."

"There's a shirt in his wardrobe next to his clean trousers. They might need a quick iron."

"Okay, okay. Got it. I don't need written instructions."

Two seconds later, my wife was kissing the kids and leaving our house in her black SUV. She forgot to kiss me, which was no big deal, though I felt left out of her affection. Once she was gone, I tried to act like I knew what I was doing. Sam and Rachel attended a local primary school that was by far the best in the county. The school's codes of conduct were so strict that every parent feared their kids would get kicked out for some minor infraction, like wearing a dirty uniform, which would mean their kids would end up going to the *second* best school, the one nobody wanted their children to go to, the school for rejects. "Okay, Sam, take off that shirt and your trousers. Chuck them in the washing machine. I'll get you some clean clothes that you'd better not dirty."

It took twenty minutes to get my son ready for the second time – as well as dressing myself in some clothes suitable for going out. My car was parked on the driveway. I pressed the button on the electronic fob to unlock the car's doors, letting Sam and Rachel jump into the back seats with their bulging backpacks that slumped over their shoulders and made them look like miniature explorers.

The grass-cutting machines had moved on, but I could hear them in the distance mowing somewhere down the street.

It was unpleasantly hot outside. The sky was a bright, cloudless blue, but there was something odd about it. There were other colours in the sky. I stopped to look upwards over the houses, noticing subtle green, red and purple patterns over my head like strands of silk shimmering in a breeze. I'd never seen the aurora borealis in real life – but the shifting lights looked just like the images I'd seen on TV. I hadn't known you could see it during the day. It was beautiful.

I entered my the car and got behind the wheel. Rachel and

Sam had noticed the strange lights in the sky. They were staring through the windows.

"Dad, what is that?" Sam said. "Is it fireworks?"

I tried explaining as I started the engine and drove out onto the road. "It's -"

Just then, there was an intense white flash from the sky. A stabbing pain hurt my eyes. I closed them in reaction, but I was left with glowing haloes on my retinas, afterimages caused by the flash.

The flash only lasted a moment – but it left me stunned. In a panic, I remembered the kids in the back. "Are you all right?"

They were both rubbing their eyes.

Rachel was moaning. "Ow! That hurt!"

Sam was blinking tears. "Dad, what was that? Was it a nuclear bomb?"

"No, no! Uh – must have been dry lightning," I said, though truthfully I had no clue. Had the flash come from space? The light show was still there, the colours pulsing across the sky. Nobody appeared hurt by the flash, but it had been disturbing. The haloes on my retinas were already fading. "It's nothing to worry about. It's just the weird weather."

My car had stopped when I hit the instinctively hit the brake during my temporary blindness. I was parked half on the driveway and half on the street. I was okay to drive on – but the car would not start.

The car appeared dead.

The dashboard normally had a dozen glowing LEDs on it even when it was turned off – but they were not functioning. The flash must have ruined the electronics. Whatever was wrong, I could not fix it. I'd have to contact the garage to have an engineer check it out – but that could wait for later. I could not leave my car parked dangerously.

"Okay, everyone out."

Sam and Rachel climbed out of the car. From the kerb, they watched me release the brake and roll the dead car out of the driveway to park it next to our house. Then I got out and closed the door. It wouldn't lock with the electronic fob – but I didn't have to worry about anyone stealing it. Nobody could drive it away.

"What are we going to do, Dad?" Rachel said. "We're supposed to be at school in twenty minutes."

Laura had trusted me to get them to school. The car was a problem I'd solve later. There was still time to get the kids to school before opening time.

"Okay, forget the car," I said. "We'll walk it."

Rachel's eyes bugged out. "Dad, you want me to *walk to school*? Can't we get a taxi, Dad? My stuff weighs a ton!"

She sounded like I'd asked her to jump out of a plane without a parachute. "You've got two feet, Rachel. You can make it. It's only a short walk. In my day I walked a mile to school every day – in rain and snow. At least it's a nice hot day. Come on, you two, let's go. You'll enjoy the exercise."

Rachel glared at me as we set off on our journey along the street. She and her brother were soon groaning under the weight of their backpacks. After only a short distance, Rachel begged me to carry her bag. I lugged it over one shoulder. It was pretty heavy. What on earth did she have in it? A couple of bricks? I was lucky Sam didn't want me to carry his backpack, too.

We were approaching the end of our street when I saw one of the grass cutting machines on the road. The engine was rumbling – but there was nobody driving it. I could not see the driver nearby. The engine was revving.

There was a pool of dark liquid on the road under the machine, running down into the drain. I assumed it was leaking oil.

As we approached, I heard a moan coming from the far side of the machine, which was the front, where the blades were whirring. It sounded like a whimpering animal.

I imagined it was a dog that had been struck. I didn't want my kids seeing that.

"Stay back," I said to Sam and Rachel. I went around the machine, afraid of what I'd find.

The air smelled coppery, like blood.

And then I saw the source of the whimpering.

It was a man. The driver. He was caught under the machine with his legs trapped. The whirring blades were chewing up his flesh and bones. He was trying to pull away – but the machine kept inching forward as though it had a mind of its own and wanted to kill him, slicing up more of his legs piece by piece, chunk by chunk. The blades had completely torn apart his feet and lower legs. There was nothing left of them, except for a spray on the vehicle and on the tarmac. The blades were now cutting into his knees. His face twisted in agony as his eyes turned to me.

"Help me! Turn it off! Turn it off! It's killing me!"

I was frozen in horror. Rachel and Sam yelled at me to do something. I listened to them and agreed. I had to help the man. What could I do? The machine was killing the man right in front of my children. How could I save him? Maybe I could stop it if I got at the controls? I'd have to climb onto it while it was bucking back and forth, grinding the man's legs into meat. I ran behind the machine and looked for a way to climb into the seat – but I didn't have enough time. As though it sensed what I intended to do, the machine pulled away from me, jolting forward, running over the injured driver, spraying his blood high in the air. He screamed and screamed. The machine drove over him, grinding its blades over his body, muffling his screams.

In shock, I watched the machine rush off down the road, leaving the driver's dead body in its wake. There wasn't much of the man's face left. Just one good eye. The other was gone. Like his nose and teeth.

Sam and Rachel sobbed.

I stared at the dead man, fumbling my phone out of my pocket. It was too late for an ambulance, but I could call 999 and report the accident. I switched it on and waited for it to get a signal – but the screen stayed blank. My phone was like my car. It was dead. The flash had fried it.

The grass cutter had gone about twenty metres when it slowed down and stopped like it had run out of petrol. Thank God for that, I thought, but then the engine roared and the machine started turning in a circle until it was facing my direction. Then it stopped, its engine idling. It reminded me of a bull waiting to launch an attack on a matador.

Rachel grabbed my arm and tugged. "Dad … it's coming to get us."

"No," I said, because I could not believe it.

There had to be a reason why the vehicle had turned around. The steering wheel must have moved, turning the wheels.

The machine wasn't alive.

It was a mindless machine.

I'd just witnessed a tragic accident.

That was what I told myself.

Not that I believed it.

I believed it had murdered that man.

That – of course – was impossible.

"What are we going to do?" Rachel whispered.

"We'll go back home," I said. "We'll be safe there. Come on."

"Dad," Sam said. "We can't go home. There's another behind us."

I looked over my shoulder and saw a second grass cutter. It was driving wildly on the verge, but it wasn't driverless. The council worker was still in his seat, grappling with the controls as it veered left and right, obviously trying to buck him off his seat. The machine, no longer under his control, was moving at about forty miles an hour. There was a thick branch from an oak tree hanging over a fence beside the verge. The machine drove under the tree, knocking the man off. The man landed on the grass and didn't move. His neck was twisted at a fatal angle.

That machine was travelling so fast it slammed into the fence and crashed through it into the woods on the other side.

At the same moment, the first machine turned on its own headlights, which were covered in the driver's blood. They looked like bloodshot eyes. Looking at me. Looking at Sam and Rachel.

It started moving towards us. The blades spun faster. Hungry for our flesh.

"Run!" I said.

We all ran down the street with the grass cutter chasing us at its maximum speed. There was nowhere to hide. On one side was the verge and the fence. On the opposite side were the high stone walls and the locked iron gates belonging to our neighbours' properties. I could probably climb over the wall – but I was not abandoning my kids. I was running out of options. Our house was too far away. We'd never make it. Not with the grass cutter charging down the road.

"This way," I said, running up to the wall. I grabbed my daughter and lifted her onto my shoulders. "Get over. Jump down on the other side. You'll be safe there."

Rachel wasted no time. She climbed over and jumped down into our neighbour's garden. Then I lifted up my son and pushed him over to safety. By then, the grass cutter was almost upon me.

"Dad!" Sam and Rachel shouted. "Climb, Dad! Climb!"

There was no time for climbing. The machine was racing at me. "Listen! Get into that house and hide. Wait for me to come to you!"

I turned and faced the machine. It intended to run me down – but I sprinted across the road a moment before it would have hit me. Its momentum carried it down the street, scraping the wall, metal screeching against the brick. It circled around to attack me again – but it could not do that until it turned around. I ran back to the black iron gates of a nearby house, shaking them, seeing they were padlocked. I would have to climb over. I grabbed the bars and climbed up the gate. I was nearly over it when the machine attacked again – heading straight for the gates, determined to crush me. I was perched on the top when the machine slammed into the gates. The gates were sturdy and held – but I fell backwards onto the machine. I landed hard on top of the engine compartment. The machine reversed, taking me with it away from the gates. The fall had momentarily stunned me. The machine did a rapid U-turn, attempting to throw me off. For a second, all I could do was hold on as the machine spun around and around in the middle of the road, trying to knock me off. I yelled and clambered into the driver's seat, looking at the controls, which were similar to a car's. I hit the brake – but nothing happened. I flicked switches. Nothing. I twisted the ignition key. Nothing. The machine was unstoppable.

It sped up, racing down the road towards the overhanging branch that had killed the second driver. If I was still seated when we got there, the branch would hit me at deadly speed.

I jumped off onto the verge, rolling and rolling.

The machine hurtled past the tree – then braked.

I got to my feet unsteadily, blood running down my leg

from cuts and bruises. I spat out a mouthful of grass cuttings. The machine was turning again.

God! Why did it want to kill me? What had the flash done to it?

I was standing close to the hole in the fence. I thought about going through it to hide in the woods – but the other machine was on that side, probably waiting for me. No – I wasn't going that way.

"Dad! This way!"

I looked at Sam and Rachel. They had somehow unlocked the gates. They were waving at me. It was all the encouragement I needed. I ran for my life. The grass cutter roared. I reached the gates just ahead of it. The machine was right behind me, blades whirring, as I got through. There was no time to close the gates. It came through at great speed. I dived to one side as the machine flew by. Before it turned around, we raced through the gates and slammed them shut. That would keep the grass cutter trapped for a while, I hoped.

We hurried home. When I heard a crack, I saw the second grass cutter knocking down a section of the fence. We raced up our driveway. I opened our front door just as the machine reached the bottom of the driveway. Sam and Rachel raced inside. I followed them. The grass cutter smashed into the door five seconds after I had locked it. It couldn't break down the door – I didn't think – but it banged against it several times before giving up. There was silence.

"Get upstairs," I told Sam and Rachel. They hurried up the stairs. I stayed in the hall and listened for the machine. I couldn't hear it – but I sensed it was out there, waiting for another chance to attack us.

I went into the living room and looked out the bay window. The machine was on the driveway, not moving. Hah! It couldn't get us now we were inside.

I thought of my wife. Worried, I turned on the TV to see if I could find out some news. But the TV was dead. I tested some lights. The flash had turned off the power supply.

I joined my kids upstairs.

Looking out of the windows, I saw the grass cutter mowing up our azaleas, probably out of frustration because it had failed to kill us. After a few minutes, other machines joined it on our lawn. One stayed on the front lawn, while the other drove around the back of our house. They had us surrounded, but we were safe for now.

Sam glared at the light show in the sky. "It's that, isn't it, Dad? It's sending them a signal to kill us, right?"

"Possibly," I said. I wondered if it was just the grass cutters or had other machines also changed.

"Dad," Rachel said. "I hear something."

"What?"

"It's in the house."

I stepped out onto the landing. I could hear it too. A humming sound. It was coming from below. I could hear something thumping on the stairs. I looked down.

No, no, no!

Something was crawling up the stairs.

It was our cordless vacuum cleaner.

Hunting us down.

SKY AND THE SPIRIT CHILD

In the summer of 1917, a young and pregnant Irish woman joined Professor Varnok's Amazing Travelling Circus with her unborn child kicking in her swollen belly. Her name was Maura O'Bryan, and she desperately needed somewhere to live.

Until then, Maura had lived her whole life in Hell's Kitchen, New York, with no hope and no dreams. The carnie folk recognised her as one of their own and welcomed her into their family as they crossed America from east to west, stopping at little towns every hundred miles to put on a grand show. Maura was too close to her due date to work hard, but she cleaned the trailers and made herself useful, grateful to have a home. Nobody asked her why she had arrived with cuts and bruises on her face, her startlingly pretty face gaunt and haunted, but they guessed she was running away from something or someone. Most people joining Professor Varnok's Amazing Travelling Circus were.

For the first time, Maura experienced the world beyond Hell's Kitchen, relishing the open sky. The sky was so big it felt like a door had opened in heaven, welcoming her soul. No longer bound to her past, Maura was free and happy, but it did not last long.

Maura gave birth on their way across South Dakota after a long and painful delivery. As soon as her baby was born, Maura named the baby Sky and held the bawling infant to her chest, weeping with joy ... but then Maura closed her eyes with a perfect smile gracing her face. Everyone present—Mrs Brady, the Cappelli sisters, Max Freeborn and Truly Trudy—knew something was wrong when Maura stopped breathing. Unknown to anyone, she had lost too much blood and had passed away.

The family did not report her death to the authorities. They buried Maura on a hill and moved on, but every year, on the anniversary of her death, they returned to South Dakota and laid flowers next to the ring of stones marking her grave.

Right away, everyone knew Sky was different from the other babies. Sky's sex remained a mystery even under close examination. Even her midwife, Mrs Brady, was not sure. Some people thought she was a girl. Some people thought he was a boy. Sky's features were both beautiful and handsome. It seemed as though people saw what they wanted to see, not what was really there. They could not even agree on the colour of Sky's eyes, hair, or skin.

For practical purposes, Sky was registered as male on the birth certificate completed by Sven Thorsson and Truly Trudy, the couple who became Sky's de facto parents. They were listed as Sky's parents and provided a home for the child, but Sky was cared for by everyone sharing the responsibility.

Professor Varnok's Amazing Travelling Circus was both mother and father to Sky, who grew up in an exciting world that was forever changing—a boisterous, wild, dangerous world, the world of the travelling circus. In the conventional world beyond its boundaries, Sky would have been forced to choose one sex or the other, boy or girl, but no decision had to be made in Professor Varnok's Amazing Travelling Circus.

Sky chose neither.

Whenever Sky looked in a mirror, the face reflected revealed itself without illusion. It lacked the solid features of a nose and brows, like a skull stripped of flesh. There was flesh, but it shimmered and dazzled, shining like moonlight. Magic or mimicry turned that flesh into a male or female face in the minds of other people, but the illusion did not work on Sky. Sky saw under the human mask and wished to see what everyone else did. A normal human face. Sky did not like seeing that glimmering creature lacking a true identity.

What am I? Sky wondered. *Am I human or something else?*

Seventeen summers followed, during which Sky became a valued member of the travelling circus, schooled in the performing arts, an adept assistant to anyone.

Sky was dressed as a girl the day she met Emily and fell instantly in love. It happened while Sky was practising knife tricks on the elephant-trampled grass outside Sven Thorsson and Truly Trudy's trailer. Emily suddenly appeared around the side of the big top while Sky was juggling six spinning knives. The girl was breathless and running, one hand holding onto her cornflower blue bonnet so it did not blow off her head, the other hand lifting the hem of her swishing long dress away from the dirt and mud. Emily saw Sky and grinned like they were sharing a secret joke, which puzzled Sky because they had never met. Sky felt an intense connection and an overwhelming desire for the running girl. Love and lust—pure and powerful. Stunned by Emily's beauty, Sky lost concentration and dropped the knives into the grass, narrowly avoiding an injury. Emily sprinted by Sky, mouthing "sorry" as she ran towards a sideshow tent. Sky realised the girl intended to hide inside the tent, but she tripped on her hem and fell over a short distance from the entrance.

A moment later, five angry teenage boys dashed into sight

in hot pursuit. They saw Emily had fallen and jeered. They were hard-faced, aged between fifteen and nineteen, all dark-haired, muscular and obviously related because they shared the same buck teeth and protruding foreheads. They looked like brothers. They were local people, not carnie folk. Emily scrambled to her feet, no doubt intending to sprint away, but she gasped as her ankle failed to support her leg. The boys caught up with her, surrounding her, pushing her back down. They kicked her and sneered. They tore at her pretty dress and ripped off her bonnet, tossing it into a pile of steaming horse manure.

"Give us the money back," one youth said, pulling at her dress, searching her roughly. "Where is it? Where's our money?"

"I dropped it," Emily said. "It's over there somewhere."

"Liar! You're hiding it. I want it. Give it back or I'll beat you to an inch of your life."

"Beat her anyway, Tommy," another said. "For cheating us."

"Yeah. We are gonna make you pay."

Sky had picked up the knives. They were fanned in Sky's left hand when Sky called to the boys. "Hey! Leave her alone."

The tallest and oldest one faced Sky and laughed. "I'm supposed to be scared of *you*? What the hell are you—a boy in a dress?"

"I'm an expert thrower of knives," Sky answered. "Would you like one in your throat?"

"I've got a knife too," the boy said. "Look."

The youth pulled a large knife. His friend sniggered. One spoke in a growl. "Gut the freak, Tommy."

Sky was not impressed. With a deft motion that defied the eyes, a knife flew and landed between the one called Tommy's feet. The boy flinched and looked scared. Sky readied another knife. "The next one will be higher. Now go!"

The gang scrabbled away. Tommy stopped at a safe distance

and snarled. "We'll get you!"

Sky glared and stepped forward. The gang fled over a field, away from the travelling circus, back towards the road leading to the nearest town, which was in upstate New York.

Emily was on her feet again, testing her ankle and wincing.

"Are you hurt bad?" Sky asked.

"No," Emily said. "Thanks for helping."

"You're welcome. I'm Sky. Pleasure to meet you." Sky offered a hand to shake. The girl accepted. Her hand was soft and warm. A pleasurable heat rose through Sky's body, looking into the girl's dark blue eyes.

"My name's Emily," the girl said.

"What was that about?"

"They lost a bet," Emily said. "Then they wanted the money back because they thought I'd cheated. I didn't. Do you think they'd come back?" She looked worried.

"They might, but I'm not scared. I can fight."

"Good! I'd better stick with you," Emily said. "You and me will be best friends."

Sky helped Emily over to her bonnet. The girl retrieved it and shook her head. "Look at the mess. My father will be furious. He'll blame me. It cost a lot of money. I'm only supposed to wear it on Sundays when we go to church. But I wanted to look good today."

"It will wash off," Sky said. "I'll get a bucket and soap."

"Thanks. You are so kind."

"Do you want me to help find the money you dropped?"

Emily chuckled. "There's no need. It's here." She reached inside the bonnet and removed several coins from a secret pocket. "I wasn't going to let them steal off me when I won it off them fair and square. They were just sore losers." She winced then and touched her ribs. "Ow. One gave me a nasty kick."

"Why don't you come with me and sit down for a few minutes? I'll clean your bonnet and you can rest. That's my home, the trailer painted purple and gold. I live there with my parents, but they are working. If those boys come looking for you, they won't find you if you're inside."

Emily accepted Sky's offer. They went into the trailer and chatted for a while, sitting on Sky's bed, which was in a small compartment. Emily told Sky that her family had just joined the travelling circus.

"It's so good to make friends with another girl my age," Emily said. "I have two sisters, but they are only little kids. Do you have any brothers or sisters?"

"No, I don't."

"That boy said something weird earlier. The one called Tommy. He said something about you being a boy in a dress, but you're clearly a girl, so why did he say that?"

"It's hard to explain. I was born … different. I look like a boy to some people, but not to you. You see me as a girl, but that's not true either. It's like an optical illusion. You see what you want to see."

"I don't understand. Are you a girl or a boy?"

"I'm both and neither. If that makes sense. I'm something else. Truly Trudy – my mother – calls it the 'dazzle'. She says lots of carnie folk used to have it, but it's rare now. It's a form of shape-shifting, though I have no control over it. Does it bother you that I'm different?"

"No," Emily said. "To me, you are just a friend who saved me from a beating. Why's your mother called *Truly* Trudy?"

"She has a special gift. She can always tell if someone is lying."

"How does she do that?"

"She just knows. People send out signals when they lie. She

can read those signals."

"I'd love to meet her. She sounds really interesting. Oh, what time is it?"

"It's three o'clock."

"I need to go now. I'd like you to come to see my show tonight. It's in the red tent at seven. Will you come and watch?"

"I won't miss it," Sky said.

"Bye," Emily said, and gave Sky an unexpected kiss on the lips that sent Sky's head spinning.

Professor Varnok's Amazing Travelling Circus looked like cheap costume jewellery in the daylight, but at night it gained a magical lustre, when the darkness came and thousands and thousands of lights switched on, coloured lights glowing like stars in the firmament, casting a glamour over the camp that drew hundreds of visitors from far and wide.

The red tent, like burning flames, shone out in the darkness, drawing an impressive crowd. A barker stood outside, shouting at the passers-by.

"Come in, come in, ladies and gentlemen! See our amazing medium contact the dead! Listen to your loved ones! Hear the words of the legendary Spirit Child!"

Sky was dressed in dark clothes and a low-brimmed hat. The hat hid Sky's face in the shadows, helping Sky avoid the attention of the crowd. That night Sky wanted to remain anonymous, in case the brothers had returned. The crowd comprised of people who believed fervently in the supernatural, as well as serious sceptics, all curious to watch the Spirit Child perform. Sky joined the crowd shuffling into the tent. It cost a nickel to enter. It was dark inside, but there was some candlelight. Ushers holding red candles guided the audience to their seats. More red candles were on the stage, which was decorated with red velvet curtains. The stage was empty until the room was full—

then a tall man appeared. He wore a black suit and spoke in a deep voice that quietened the crowd. His dark eyes flickered in the candlelight.

"Ladies and gentlemen, you are gathered here tonight to witness the mighty powers of the Spirit Child. Please welcome her!"

A powerful light suddenly lit up a girl who had not been visible a moment earlier. It was Emily–of course–wearing a white lace gown that made her ghostly and angelic. She was sitting on a large wooden chair painted black. It looked like she was sitting on a dark throne.

Sky heard some sceptics whispering.

The tall man spoke again. "The Spirit Child must have complete silence to concentrate her powers."

A hushed silence fell over the audience.

And then the show began.

Emily looked into the audience and pointed at a woman. "You. Have we met before?"

"No," the woman said.

"You recently suffered a great loss, didn't you … Claire?"

The woman looked stunned that the Spirit Child knew her name. "Yes, I did."

"I'm seeing a young child. His name is … Charlie. He's here for you, Claire. He watches over you. Charlie wants you to know it did not hurt. He's happy now. He wants you to be happy, too. Do not blame yourself for the accident. It was nobody's fault, Claire."

Tears streamed down the woman's face. She sobbed into the shoulder of her husband.

"I'm now seeing a man called William. Does anyone know a William?"

Several hands shot up and the act continued.

Star grinned. *William? Everyone knew at least one William.*

As the Spirit Child, Emily continued with her act, revealing personal messages from long-lost relatives to her enraptured audience. She was good. Very good. If Star had not known how it was done, Star would have believed Emily was genuinely talking to the dead and not faking it. Star knew many mediums employed assistants disguised as normal people to learn information about their audience while they waited to take their seats. They eavesdropped and extracted personal information in conversations, which they used to make the audience believe the medium was hearing the dead speak. Most of those mediums guessed the details and made mistakes that they hastily covered up. The good ones were more subtle. They avoided making mistakes and guessed more accurately. The best ones were flawless. They not only avoided making mistakes, but they seemed to know things nobody could have told them. Emily was one of those talented few. She seemed to know so many personal, private things that she had the whole audience soon believing she was really in contact with the dead. Sky was impressed by Emily's skill.

"You, sir. The man wearing spectacles in the fourth row. You have a question?"

"My pa died last year. I never found his will, though I know he wrote one. Do you know where it is?"

"Yes. He's telling me it is in his desk. There's a secret compartment. Look underneath. There's a little latch under the left leg, near where you scratched the words 'I hate apples' when you were seven years old. Do you remember that?"

"God, yes! I never told anyone that!"

Sky wondered what would happen when the man returned home and discovered there wasn't a will in the desk. By then, the travelling circus would be in the next town, so it did not matter too much, though Sky was curious. A medium could probably not visit a town for several years if they made up too many lies.

For two hours, Sky astounded her audience. They left convinced of her supernatural powers. Only Sky knew it was all fake. Sky waited until the tent was empty before going up to see Emily. Emily removed her white gown, under which she was wearing her ordinary dress. They slipped out of the back of the tent and walked towards the lion cages under the starry night sky. They sat down on the cool grass and watched the shooting stars.

"You were excellent," Sky said. "How did you know about that man's hatred of apples?"

Emily smiled and looked straight into Sky's eyes. "A spirit told me. His grandfather."

"Come on. Tell me the truth. Was the man a plant in the audience?"

Emily stopped smiling and scowled. She jumped to her feet. "Sky, do you think I'm a fake?"

"Well, yes, obviously. I grew up in the carnie. I know how it is done. There are no such things as a genuine medium. I know how it works."

"You know how *most* people do it," she said angrily. "Not me! I am a genuine psychic!"

"Emily, I didn't mean to upset you, but don't lie to me."

"I'm not lying! Do you want me to *prove* it?"

"No," Sky said, realising Emily was furious. "Forget I said anything. Let's not talk about it."

"You're sceptical. You think I'm a liar. Very well. I don't like doing this uninvited, but I will prove I'm psychic." Emily stared intensely at Sky, her dark blue eyes seeming to darken to black. "I can see a beautiful woman standing behind you. She has long, black hair and blue eyes. Her name is Maura O'Bryan. She died giving birth to you, just after giving you your name."

Sky jumped up, angry and confused. "How did you know that? Did someone tell you?"

"Yes," Emily said. "*She* did."

Sky didn't believe her. It was a trick. A cruel trick. Truly Trudy had told the truth about Sky's real mother when Sky was old enough to understand – but it was a secret nobody outside the travelling circus knew. Everyone else was supposed to think Sven Thorsson and Truly Trudy were Sky's birth parents. For a newcomer to know Sky's birth mother was Maura O'Bryan came as a huge shock. Either someone had betrayed Sky's privacy or Emily really could see and hear the dead, which was something Sky struggled to believe.

"If you really are psychic, tell me where she's buried and what I do there every year."

Emily was quiet for a minute, looking like she was listening to someone standing behind Sky. "She says she died in South Dakota. She's buried under a ring of rocks. You visit her grave with pink and yellow peonies."

That was something nobody else knew.

"I can't believe it," Sky said. "You really are psychic?"

"It should not be too surprising for you. You were born different, too."

"That's true," Sky admitted. They were alike. "What else can you do? Can you see the future?"

"No – but sometimes the dead will tell me something that might happen." Emily looked at a spot over Sky's right shoulder and tilted her head slightly, listening and nodding. "Yes. Yes. I will..."

Sky felt left out of the conversation. "What is my mother saying now?"

"She's telling me an address. The Garamond Building in New York. Apartment 522."

"What's there?"

Emily hesitated. "I can't ask her."

"Why not?"

"She's gone."

"Gone? Gone *where*?"

"Spirits move on once they have finished with our world. I think she stayed to give you that message. I can't see sense her presence any longer. I'm sorry, Sky."

"I don't understand. Did she want me to *go* to that address or *avoid* it?"

Emily sighed. "I don't know why. But New York's not too far from here. You could get there on a train. It would only take an hour. You could go tomorrow. I'll come with you if you like. You can visit the address with me. What do you say?"

Sky had never gone far beyond the travelling circus's boundary, no matter where they travelled. The idea of travelling to New York frightened Sky because it was so full of strangers. New York was a giant city, a daunting place. Sky thought about Emily's offer to come along. "I'll do it because I'm curious. Emily, I'd like your company very much."

"Great!" Emily said. "I'll see you in the morning at breakfast!"

They said goodbye and parted.

Sky was ready to go to bed for the night – but as Sky crossed the camp, something moved in the darkness ahead, near the trailer where Sky lived. Someone was hiding around the side of a sideshow tent, watching the area where Sky had been that morning throwing knives. Only the hidden figure's slight movement against the darker background of the night sky had alerted Sky to the threat. Sky crept closer, approaching the figure from behind. In the cold lights of the stars, a face became visible. It was the oldest teenager – Tommy – hunched down, holding a

Louisville slugger in both hands. Waiting to ambush Sky.

"Looking for me?" Sky said, taking delight in surprising the boy, who spun around, swinging the bat at empty air. Sky had danced backwards, effortlessly avoiding the attack. Before Tommy swung a second time, Sky disarmed him with a high kick, knocking the bat out of Tommy's grip. Enraged, the boy charged like a bull–but Sky dodged aside, tripping him over. Tommy landed on his face in the dirt. Sky picked up the bat and poked Tommy in the back, keeping him down when he tried to get back up. Sky was tempted to use the bat, breaking some bones or at least giving the thug some bruises to remember, but the local police would close down the travelling circus if someone from the town was beaten by a carnie. Locals always sided with their own. A stern warning would have to be enough.

"Listen good," Sky said. "You're not welcome here. Next time I see you, I'll break your kneecaps. Do you understand?"

"Yes," Tommy muttered.

"Then get lost and never come back."

Tommy scrambled off.

Sky twirled the bat, laughing.

Sky doubted Tommy would come back again.

When Sky entered the trailer, Truly Trudy and Sven Thorsson were cavorting half-naked on a couch. They didn't stop when they saw Sky, who was used to their amorous displays. Truly Trudy was kissing Sven's big hairy face until she noticed the Louisville slugger.

"Sky, I did not know you liked baseball."

"Oh, I thought I'd give it a go."

Truly Trudy frowned. She knew what Sky had said was a lie. "Sky, you did not hurt someone, did you?"

"No," Sky said.

Truly Trudy looked relieved, though she continued to

frown. "Who gave you that bat?"

"I ... took it from a local who wanted to cause trouble. It's nothing to worry about. I scared them off."

"You had better throw that thing away," Truly Trudy said. "If the police come here, we don't want them accusing you of stealing."

Sky had wanted to keep the bat to use in a juggling routine, but Truly Trudy was right. "I'll throw it away in the morning. I'm tired, Ma. I'll go to bed now."

"Don't forget," Truly Trudy said, giggling as her husband kissed her neck and caressed her ample cleavage.

"I won't forget," Sky promised, before going to bed, leaving the bat resting against the wall.

The next morning, Sky dumped the baseball bat into a muddy ditch outside the camp before eating breakfast with Emily. Emily was wearing a pretty red dress and looked beautiful. For the journey into New York, Sky had opted for a man's grey coat, pants and a cap.

"I have a show tonight," Emily said. "But I have all day to get back here. Stretch says he will give us a ride to the station."

Stretch was the seven-foot-eight strongman. He gave Sky and Emily a ride in his car and told them he would come back for them at four o'clock, which gave them plenty of time to go to New York and return.

The train journey was exciting, but also uneventful. Sky loved looking out of the windows as little towns rushed past at what seemed like incredible speed. It was raining when Sky saw New York rising like a silver mountain ahead. The Empire State Building was an awe-inspiring sight, even in the rain. It had just been completed in 1931. It was the tallest building in the world. Sky stared at it until it disappeared behind other buildings near Grand Central on 42nd Street. Before leaving the station, Sky and

Emily bought an umbrella that they shared as they walked to the Garamond Building in the heavy rain.

Their destination was an impressive apartment building facing Central Park. They stopped opposite it and observed a doorman standing at the entrance.

"Hell. We can't ask to be let in if we don't know who lives there," Sky said. "I don't suppose a spirit could tell you?"

"No. Spirits are not like encyclopaedias waiting to be asked questions."

"I suppose I could sneak past him if you provided a distraction. Will you do that?"

Emily nodded. "Give me the umbrella. I'll cross the street and distract the doorman. Slip inside when he's not watching."

"What about you?"

"I'll wait here for you."

Emily crossed the road and *accidentally* tripped and lost hold of her umbrella. The chivalrous doorman came to her assistance, while Sky slipped into the building's lobby. An Otis elevator was next to the stairs. There was likely to be an operator inside, so Sky climbed the stairs up to the fifth floor. Apartment 522 had a white door. Sky heard music playing on the other side. It sounded like Mozart. Shy knocked loud enough to be heard over the music and waited. The music ended abruptly as a needle was taken off a gramophone. Sky knocked again.

"I'm coming!" a man said.

The door was opened by a stout, bald man in a red silk robe. He was sweating profusely, his head covered in beads of perspiration. He stared at Sky, keeping his loose robe closed over his potbelly with both pudgy hands. He was in his fifties, and he was breathing heavily like he had been doing something strenuous. Behind the big man, Sky glimpsed someone naked flit from one room to another, a voluptuous young woman with short black hair and long legs. She was gone like a ghost in the blink of an eye. The bald man stared at Sky, gathering his breath.

"Yes?" he said.

"Uh, I'm looking for someone living here."

"This is my apartment," the man said. "What do you want?"

"My mother gave me address. Have you heard of Maura O'Bryan?"

"Never heard of her," the man said. "You've got the wrong address. Goodbye."

"But -"

The door was closing when the woman reappeared wearing a white bathrobe. "Stop, George! Let our visitor in."

George reluctantly opened the door for Sky. He mumbled something as the woman walked towards Sky. The woman was very beautiful and half George's age. She stared at Sky and told George to make some coffee. Then she invited Sky to sit down on a leather couch. She introduced herself as Dee.

"Your mother is Maura O'Bryan?"

"Was. She died."

"Oh. I didn't know. That's terrible."

"You knew her?"

"I did."

"Were you her friend?"

Dee smiled sadly. "Not exactly. I'm your father."

"My father?" The news came as a surprise, but not as a shock. Sky studied the face of Dee and noticed a subtle glow, like when Sky looked in a mirror. "You're like me. You can be a man or a woman. You have the dazzle."

"The dazzle? Is that what you call it? I like that. Yes – I have the dazzle. George sees me as a woman – but your mother saw me as a man. What do I look like to you?"

"A beautiful young woman."

"That's interesting. I always wondered what one of my kind would see. I've never met anyone else like me. My parents died when I was an infant. They were faerie folk. I grew up in the human world feeling alone – until I met your mother."

Sky had a question. "What do you see when you look at me?"

"Does it matter?"

"No," Sky said, realising it didn't. "Can I ask you something else?"

"Yes. Anything."

"Did you love my mother?"

"Yes. With all of my heart."

"If you loved her, why did you hurt her?"

"*Hurt?* I never hurt her, I swear."

"Truly Trudy—my adopted mother—told me she had bruises when she first saw her. Somebody beat her. If she wasn't running from you, tell me what happened?"

"I'd better start at the beginning. They found me as a baby in an alley in Hell's Kitchen, next to the dead bodies of my parents. They had been killed by a mob who thought they were abominations because of their changing faces. I was taken in by a childless couple called Robert and Alice. They were from Ireland and realised I had faerie blood – but they loved me and treated me as their own child. They protected me from their superstitious neighbours. Your mother lived down my block with her family. We liked each other from the first time we met. As children, we played together. Years later, we became more than friends and fell in love. Unfortunately, her father caught us together in a romantic situation. He was furious because he saw me as a girl and thought his own daughter was a sexual deviant. He threatened to kill me and banned her from ever seeing me, but we continued meeting in secret. We planned to leave New

York when we had the money for a journey to California, but then Maura confided our plans to her sister, Rose, who told her father. He beat her and intended to shoot me with a gun. To save me, Maura hit him over the head with a brick. It killed him. Your mother ran away to avoid being arrested for his murder." Deed sighed. "I never did find out where she went. I would have gone anywhere to see her again, but she never sent me a letter."

Dee's story stunned Sky. "I think she would have contacted you when she got to California if she had not died giving birth to me."

Dee nodded. "You must tell me all about yourself."

"I will," Sky said. "But my friend's outside in the rain. Do you mind if she comes in and joins us?"

"Not at all," Dee said. "George, darling, will you find the young lady?"

That morning, Sky told Dee all about life in Professor Varnok's Amazing Travelling Circus. They also spent the afternoon getting to know each other. Sky liked Dee and wanted to stay all day, but they had to get back for the evening show.

"The travelling circus is staying in New York until Sunday," Sky said. "I'd like you to visit us before we go."

"I wouldn't miss it," Dee said.

Sky sighed. "We have to leave now to catch our train."

"Leave now? Nonsense. I have a better idea. I'm not saying goodbye just yet. George and I will take you back in our car. Sky, I want to meet your family and see the travelling circus today."

Two hours later, it was still raining when they arrived at Professor Varnok's Amazing Travelling Circus in George's black car. Sky introduced Dee to Truly Trudy and Sven Thorsson and then showed Dee and George around the travelling circus, introducing the rest of the family.

That evening Sky performed an acrobatic juggling act in the big top in front of a large crowd that included Dee and George. Afterwards, Sky went outside alone to cool down in the rain while other acts performed. Sky intended to go back in a minute to spend more time with Dee, but someone hit Sky from behind and laughed as Sky slumped semi-conscious.

"Hope that hurt, freak."

Even in a confused state, Sky recognised the voice of Tommy. He had come back with his brothers. And they all had baseball bats. They rained blows down on Sky until the pain was the only thing in existence. And then they dragged Sky away from the bright lights into the darkness.

They were a long way from Professor Varnok's Amazing Travelling Circus when they stopped. Nobody could hear Sky cry out as the brothers used their baseball bats. Sky moaned in pain, wishing the beating would end. Tommy grinned in the moonlight. His knife appeared. "I'm gonna cut your throat, freak."

"Er ... Tommy," one of his brothers said. "We don't need to kill nobody. That's murder. I ain't doing no murder."

The other brothers murmured in agreement. They wanted to leave, but Tommy snarled at them. "Nobody's going home until this freak is dead and buried."

"I ain't sticking around for that!" his brother said and ran off. The others did the same, leaving Tommy on his own.

"Cowards," Tommy muttered. "Looks like I'll have to do this by myself."

Tommy towered over Sky with the knife shining against the background of the stars.

The edge was so sharp, so deadly.

Tommy bent down to cut Sky's throat.

Sky was too weak to even raise a hand to block the knife as

Tommy's knife slashed sideways and–

Suddenly it stopped an inch from Sky's neck.

"What the–" Tommy muttered, eyes widening in confusion.

And then he screamed.

Hours later, Sky woke in another place. A bed. Truly Trudy was there, pressing an ice pack to Sky's bruises. Dee was there, too. And so was Emily, looking scared.

"Is Sky going to be all right?"

"Yes," Truly Trudy said. "In a few days."

Sky tried speaking, but it hurt too much to say anything longer than two words. "What happened?"

"Dee saved your life," Emily said. "With the help of your mother. She came to me again and told me you were in danger. She told us where to find you. I told Dee, and we raced over just in time. Dee broke that boy's wrist and knocked him out with one punch."

"I couldn't let him harm you," Dee said.

Emily nodded. "George tied him up and locked him in the trunk of his car. George is taking him for a long ride. By the time he finds his way back, we will all be long gone."

"George and I have decided to come along for a few weeks," Dee said. "It's too early to say goodbye."

Sky would have grinned if it had not hurt to move a muscle. Emily sat down beside Sky, squeezing a hand. Dee sat on the other side, doing the same thing.

Surrounded by loved ones, Sky went to sleep, knowing the next day would be a good one, rain or shine.

LITTLE MONSTER

Deep in the bayou, the murky green water rippled in the moonlight as Clayton Mooney's small sports fishing boat slipped stealthily up the river. The three men aboard were brothers dressed like anglers, but none were hunting for fish that night. You did not need guns for that. Eli and Zeke watched the river while Clayton steered to the GPS coordinates given to him by Smoky Petersson. Clayton did not know what he was picking up for his boss – he was not paid to ask dumb questions – but he knew it had to be tonight when the moon was full. He didn't need any lights to see – which was crucial to remaining unseen by the local cops. Sheriff Jessup was always looking for smugglers. A dozen of the guys Clayton had gone to school with had been busted in the last year because someone spotted them from the shore. They were all in prison, serving long sentences. He didn't want to join them.

"Are we there yet?" Eli said, sounding like a little kid, not a seventeen-year-old with a thick black beard down to his navel.

Clayton shook his head. "Ten minutes."

"I got classes in the morning, bro."

Clayton grinned to himself. *Classes? Like the boy would ever graduate high school.* Clayton loved his youngest brother – but Eli was as thick as his momma's molasses. The kid thought Kentucky was just a flavour of chicken.

"We'll be home in time for breakfast," Clayton promised. "Dump some chum, Eli. Get the fish excited."

There was a cooler on the deck filled with raw meat. Wearing black rubber gloves, Eli tossed some over the side. Clayton heard it splash into the water. The smell of the blood would attract the bigger predators for miles – keeping them away from where they were heading.

Clayton stared at the dark water ahead, listening to the sounds of the bullfrogs and gators, feeling a cool breeze on his face that smelled like decaying flowers. Something bumped against the boat and rocked it.

"Jeez!" Eli said. "What was that?"

"Probably a gator," Clayton said.

"Oh, man. I don't like this. I HATE gators."

Zeke chuckled. "Clay, I told you not to bring him. He's scared of his own shadow. Could have done this by ourselves, split the money two ways."

"I ain't scared," Eli said. "I was just asking, is all. Ain't I allowed to ask stuff? I ain't never done nothing like this. You guys have been doing it for years."

"It's fine to ask questions," Clayton said. "It's the only way of learning. Just keep your voice down, Eli. Voices have a way of carrying over the bayou. We don't want the sheriff and his deputies hearing us tonight. Just keep watch, Eli. No talking unless you see something."

"Okay, Clay. Whatever you say. I ain't saying nothing. Not me. No. I'm gonna be real quiet, like a mouse. I -"

"Shut up," Zeke snarled.

Eli stopped talking.

Five minutes later, the GPS was showing they had arrived at the location, which was in a wide section of the river about five miles north of Grady's Landing. Beyond that little town were the Gulf of Mexico and the probable source of the package they were collecting. Clayton switched off the engine and coasted to a stop. The water was deep here – but it was also clear half of the way down to the bottom. In the moonlight the catfish were active, coming up to the surface, their mouths gasping for air before they dived back under and vanished into the gloom. Clayton saw some big ones. If he didn't have a job to do, he would have liked to have done some night fishing, catching something for their momma's gumbo pot. But he had to concentrate now. It was already after midnight.

"Zeke, it's time to put on your wetsuit."

His brother stripped to his shorts and slipped into his wetsuit and scuba gear. Clayton checked over his oxygen tank and mask before tapping him on the back and wishing him luck. Zeke lowered himself into the water without causing a ripple. Clayton handed him a line. Zeke gave a thumbs-up and dived, taking the line down with him to attach to the package. Zeke had a small powerful flashlight strapped on his head – but he would not turn it on until he was at the bottom. Clayton leant over the side and watched his brother descend into the darkness. Zeke slowly vanished.

Eli stood beside him, staring down. "What do we do?"

"We wait for the signal to pull it up."

"Dude, can I text Jolene?"

"No," Clayton said. "You were supposed to leave your phone behind."

"Sorry. I forgot." A sheepish grin. "Can I check Instagram and Twitter?"

"No. And you'd better not tweet about what we're doing tonight. Or take photographs of us out here breaking the law. I don't want to feature on *Criminals Do The Silliest Things*."

The guilty look on his brother's face suggested that Eli had been thinking about taking some pictures on his phone. Their momma must have been drinking heavily when she conceived Eli. The fool had no sense.

"I ain't stupid, Clay. I wasn't gonna do nothing like that, I swear. There's got to be something I can do. I mean, you wanted me to come. So, I want to be useful and learn the business."

"You can be useful by keeping watch for the police. I need your younger eyes and better hearing. Look and listen and behave like a pro."

"Look and listen. Got it."

Clayton wished he had not started working for Smoky Petersson. Ten years ago, when he had been Eli's age, he had wanted to go to college and make something good out of his life – but his dad had owed some bad folks $150,000 in gambling losses. They had threatened to beat his dad if he didn't pay them – then chop him up into gator bait if he still didn't pay. To save his old man's life, Clayton had gone to Smoky Petersson and begged him to help. He was the Dixie Mafia's man in Grady's Landing. Smoky Petersson paid off the debt and made sure nobody in Grady's Landing ever accepted a bet from his dad ever again, but Clayton made a deal with the devil. He would forever be in Smoky Petersson's debt – at his beck and call, day or night, like a slave. Two years after making the deal, his dad died anyway – killed in a bar fight over an argument about a football game.

Now Clayton looked after for his whole family – Momma, Zeke, Eli, and his little sister Candice. His primary source of income was from smuggling, which earned him more in a month than his legitimate job as a tour guide did in a year. He had never wanted to bring Zeke and Eli into the smuggling business – but Zeke had volunteered to work with him because he needed the money for his wife and ex-wife, who both had two little kids to look after. Eli had joined them because he wanted to buy a fast car to impress his girlfriend. Tonight would pay for that. They were earning $20,000 for the deal. It was easy money – so why did Clayton feel so uneasy?

Something was bothering him more than usual. It had nothing to do with the morality of being a criminal. Or the danger of getting caught. No – it was something else. The bayou seemed different. Too quiet. Yes – that was it. He could no longer hear the gators. They had gone silent. The only sounds were the distant calls of the bullfrogs across the bayou and the soft lapping of water against the boat. Why was it so quiet?

Clayton shivered and looked at his wristwatch. Zeke had been underwater for ten minutes. It should not have taken that long to find the package. What was keeping Zeke down there?

A slow cloud passed over the moon, plunging the bayou into total darkness. Clayton listened. It was even quieter. Not even the catfish were making a sound. Peering down into the black water, he thought he detected an ethereal greenish glow from deep in the depths. It had to be Zeke's head-mounted flashlight sweeping over the bottom where the water was soupy with plankton and river detritus. At least he knew Zeke was still looking for the package.

"Clay?" Eli said.

"What?"

"It's too dark. I can't see nothing. Can I turn on my phone for the light?"

"No. Let your eyes adjust to the dark."

The cloud cleared the moon and the moonlight shone on the water again. For a second Clayton was sure he had seen something moving under the boat – but he blinked and lost it. Could have been a large catfish.

Just then, he felt a tug on the line.

"About time," he muttered. "Help me pull it up, Eli."

They pulled up the line until something appeared below them. It looked black in the water – but when it reached the surface, he could see it was orange and made of hard plastic. It was a large cooler, like the one storing the chum. Zeke had hooked his line to it through the handles. Eli held onto the line so Clayton could hook the cooler and pull it to the boat's side. They both reached down and hauled it onto the deck. It was heavy, like it had been weighed down with rocks. Clayton had been told not to open it – but he wondered if it contained drugs or money or something else, like guns or a dead body. There was no way of learning what kind of thing Smoky Petersson did for the Dixie mafia without getting into serious trouble. There was a thick padlock on the cooler just to stop temptation. Clayton was grateful for it. If Smoky Peterssen even *suspected* he had looked inside, Clayton knew he would end up at the bottom of the bayou wrapped in chains, missing his head, hands and feet.

"Drag it out of sight and put a tarp over it, Eli."

"Okay."

Now they had to wait for his brother. Eli would have to take his time coming up if he wanted to avoid getting the bends. Clayton could see a light shining upwards as his brother ascended. It was getting brighter and brighter.

He could see something else in the water. Something was down there. Moving. Moving towards Zeke's light. A black thing. Long. Sleek.

"What the hell is that?" Eli said.

Clayton didn't know – but he was worried for his brother. Had Zeke noticed the danger? Clayton wished Eli had a way of contacting him on his radio – but the scuba gear didn't have audio. He waved his hands and hoped his brother could see him giving him a warning as the huge black thing swam for him.

Was it a gator?

No.

It was too big.

It was as long as his boat.

Possibly longer.

And it was heading straight for his brother.

Clayton wanted to shout a warning – but the sound would not reach his brother. The thing was partially illuminated in the beam and the moonlight. He saw scaly fins and jagged teeth.

"Do something!" Eli said.

If light attracted the thing, maybe he could distract it with another one, a brighter source?

Clayton opened the emergency box and grabbed a glow stick. They often used them for night diving. He broke it and shook it so the two chemicals mixed and reacted, getting hot, producing a bright white light that stung his eyes. He hurled the glow stick into the air away from his brother's position and hoped that, when it hit the water, the splash and bright light would distract the creature's attention.

The glow stick landed forty feet away, close to the bank. It sank under the surface, lighting the area around it like daylight. Everything lurking under the water – catfish, eels, crawfish and turtles – scattered from the light as the creature was fully illuminated.

It looked like a giant shark – the biggest shark he had ever seen, far bigger than a great white. But sharks didn't go this far up the river. It looked like a relic from another time – something prehistoric and never seen before by a living human.

Clayton remembered seeing something like it in a dinosaur book he had read as a teenager. The name popped into his head.

It was a megalodon – a species of shark stockier and much larger than a great white. They had existed millions of years ago. They were supposed to be extinct – but at least one had survived.

And it was here. In the bayou.

It was almost upon his brother, its huge jaws opened wide enough to devour him whole, when it suddenly veered off in the direction of the glow stick.

Clayton's boat rocked as the tail whipped along the underside and knocked it sideways. Clayton heard Eli gasp as the shark's body flickered past Zeke and caught him with a glancing blow that sent him tumbling back down into the darkness.

A moment later, the creature swallowed the glow stick and broke the surface, a giant dorsal fin spraying water into the air. A vile smell – like a thousand dead things rotting in a grave – wafted over the boat as the shark-like thing thrashed and turned. The rancid odour made Clayton and Eli cough. Clayton tasted sulphur.

A dark eye the size of a dinner plate shone wetly in the moonlight.

Clayton felt the intelligent mind behind it studying him. The shark started circling the boat – the huge eye staring straight at Clayton. Hungry and angry.

Remembering his gun, which he had brought along in case he encountered trouble of a more human kind, Clayton pulled it from his jacket and fired three or four shots at the creature's huge eye.

His bullets struck the water and skipped off the thick skin – harmlessly. His next shot was more accurate – striking very close to the eye. Eli started shooting too as the creature submerged its head and disappeared. Clayton stopped shooting to reload. He doubted his gun would do much against that monster – but it had not liked him shooting at its eye.

Eli was scrambling across the deck, looking for Zeke and the creature. He had his phone out and he was looking at the screen, trying to zoom in on whatever was out there.

"Where's it gone? Where's Zeke?"

There was no green light down there any longer.

Did that mean Zeke had turned off his flashlight?

Was he still alive?

Clayton could not abandon his brother if there was even a tiny chance of him being alive. Think! The first glow stick had worked. He had another eleven in his box. He hurled another one as far as possible. It landed with a soft splash.

Daylight burned under the water as the glow stick dropped to the bottom and lit up the riverbed, casting an eerie light overhead.

Like the first time, the light drew the megalodon towards it.

A splash on the other side of the boat made Clayton's heart jolt. A hand appeared over the side and his brother's head followed it as Zeke pulled himself aboard and flopped on the deck, gasping and wheezing.

"Go!" he said.

Clayton ran to the cabin and started the engine.

Eli was looking down at the frothy water. "It ate the glow stick. It's coming back now. I know what to do!"

Clayton didn't have time to wonder what his youngest brother was doing because he had to drive them out of there. Now. The problem was the boat was slow to start, and the megalodon was capable of splitting the hull.

"Hurry!" Zeke shouted.

"I'm trying! I'm trying!"

Clayton heard a whoosh as something landed in the water. Turning his head, he saw Eli holding onto the side. "I got it! I got it!"

There was a crashing impact that pushed the boat up and dropped it down hard, jolting every bone in Clayton's body. It was a miracle he stayed on his feet.

"Start, damn you."

The engine kicked into full power and Clayton pushed the lever forward, jerking the boat towards the muddy bank. He nearly crashed into it, but he swerved before impact.

The next moment, they were racing away from the megalodon, which seemed to have vanished.

Clayton didn't slow down until they were in sight of home.

Eli was grinning. "Knew that would hurt it."

"What did you do?"

"I dropped the cooler into its mouth. Made it choke on that sucker."

"You threw *my* cooler, right? The one filled with chum? You are talking about that cooler, aren't you? Not the one belonging to Smoky Petersson, right?"

Eli stopped smiling. "Did I do the wrong thing?"

WHEN THE BOUGH BREAKS

When I arrived at Arn Bunderson's tree farm, the snow was red and pink around what remained of his corpse. As I walked around the crime scene taking photographs, I vowed I'd solve Arn's murder before Christmas Day, less than a week away. It was the least I could do for his wife and kids. I'd never seen anything as horrific.

Arn's body was in a snowy field between his ranch and the tree farm, not far from the natural forest on the edge of his property. His head looked like a crushed tomato. The flattened skull had no eyes in it. They were ten feet from his body in different directions – popped out of their sockets by a powerful impact of something nasty, like a sledgehammer. Chunks of Arn's brain tissue were splattered everywhere like pieces of raw chicken.

Weirdly, the rest of him remained untouched.

Just his head had been pulped.

I saw no footprints in the snow, but a deep furrow extended from the body to the forest in a straight line. The impression was about three feet wide and possibly made by a snowmobile, but it was smooth and trackless.

Dr Melissa Greenberg – Barker County's coroner – had been examining the body for twenty minutes. We'd both been cheerleaders in high school and rivals for the hottest boys on the football team, but that had been over thirty years ago before our lives became serious. We had an awkward relationship because she had married Shane – my ex-husband, who shared joint custody of our thirteen-year-old daughter Hanna. I heard her knees cracking as she stood up, huffing, her nose and cheeks reddened by the cold.

"Sheriff, I'm ready to move him to the morgue."

"Great. It looks obvious, but I gotta ask. What's the cause of death?"

She shrugged and looked at me wearily. "What do you think? Something very heavy hit his head, completely crushing his skull, driving his spinal column into his chest. He would have been killed instantly, but I can't state with any certainty the nature of the object. The impact had to be severe to eject his eyeballs. I've honestly seen nothing like that."

Neither had I in the twenty years I'd been a cop for Barker County. "The perp left no weapon behind. What should I be looking for – a baseball bat or something?"

"Beats me."

"Best guess?"

"I don't do guesses, Sheriff."

"Melissa, I need some help here. It's obviously not Wile E. Coyote dropping an anvil off a cliff, so what do you think killed him?"

"You want my educated opinion, Sheriff?"

"I'd appreciate it."

"The last time I saw a dead body like this was in 2005 when Hal Rudd got killed during that really terrible thunderstorm."

"I don't remember that. What happened to him?"

"Lightning struck a tree. The trunk fell on him, but there's no tree here, so that's impossible."

"Shame there's no tree," I said. "I could do with a simple accident. Poor Arn. How long's he been dead?"

"Liver temp suggests three hours."

That was around four that morning. His wife Linda had found the body at seven-thirty. I looked at the dark line of the forest, then back at the Bundersons' ranch, which was decorated with cheerful Christmas lights, a big plastic Santa and a dozen glowing reindeer. Every year Arn spent days making his home look like a magical wonderland. Why would anyone want to kill a harmless family guy like him?

At this time of year, Arn Bunderson made money selling his Christmas trees. A week ago I'd bought one from him for my living room – a beautiful 9ft spruce. Normally, Arn had a whole load of them in the back of his truck, but I could see it was empty. Was that why he'd been killed? Had someone stolen his Christmas trees? Why not steal the truck, too?

I'd have to ask his wife some questions, but Linda Bunderson was being treated by a paramedic for the shock of finding her husband dead. Questioning her could wait. I was more worried about the weather. The sky was overcast and I expected more snow, potentially ruining my crime scene. Quickly, I had to finish photographing the scene before it snowed again.

I circled the area several times in wider and wider circles, looking for evidence. Each time I stepped on fresh snow, I noticed a large number of pine needles sticking to my boots. They thickly covered the snow in a layer of them all around the crime scene, but the layer thinned out after a short distance. I also found a lot of twigs and branches – some with blood on them. I bagged them in case the blood didn't match the victim.

With luck, I'd get the killer's DNA.

One of my deputies – a young and fit rookie called Sam Rodriguez – emerged from the forest. "Ma'am, I followed the snow track as best as I could, but it just stopped at a tree. What do you want me to do now?"

"Help Dr Greenberg move the body."

"Yes, ma'am."

Ma'am? That made me feel ancient. It depressed me. I had a couple of years before hitting the big 5-0. Inside, I was still as fit and healthy as a cheerleader, feeling like the only one with a gun and the physical skills to kick ass.

I sucked in a deep breath, smelling pine sap in the air, feeling the cold in my bones. A strong wind blew in from the east, making me shiver.

I walked back to the ranch.

Linda was sitting in her kitchen sipping a steaming coffee. She stared at me with dead eyes, barely aware of her surroundings, as I asked questions, establishing a timeline.

"I woke at seven. Arn had already got up earlier. I had a shower and dressed, then tried to call Arn to see if he wanted me to make him breakfast, but he didn't answer. I knew he'd be out cutting down some trees to take into town, so I … so I went to the door and looked for him. I saw him lying in the snow. I thought he'd had a heart attack or stroke. Until I got closer. Then I … I saw his head. God. What kind of sick monster would do that?"

"You didn't approach the body?"

"No. From a mile away, I could see he was dead. I didn't want to go nearer. I called you guys straight away."

"You did the right thing. Linda, did Arn have any enemies or arguments?"

"No."

"Can you think of any reasons why someone would kill him?"

"No."

My gut instinct told me she hadn't killed him. Linda was too small to smash her husband's skull with so much force.

"Linda, it's not a good idea to stay here during the investigation. Have you got somewhere you can go?"

"I'll take Ben and Emily to my sister's. Thank God they're too young to understand what's happened to their daddy."

Everyone had enemies. Even good people. Especially good people. A lot of bad people envied them. But I couldn't find anyone with a good motive for killing Arn Bunderson. It would take weeks for all of the forensic evidence to be analysed, so I decided to send my deputies to talk to his friends and family while I checked on his neighbours to see if they'd seen or heard anything unusual. By noon I'd found no witnesses or suspects. I was at a dead end.

Feeling hangry, I stopped at Jem's Diner on Main Street for coffee and cronuts and use of the free wi-fi. I logged my laptop onto the criminal database. I was looking at a long list of all the ex-felons living in my county when I got a call from Dispatch reporting on a single-vehicle crash on Vanhaven Road.

I arrived at the scene ten minutes later. An ambulance was already there – but the paramedics had nothing to do. One walked over to me, shaking his head.

"Sheriff, the driver's dead. It's Tom Chandler."

He was the owner of the biggest logging company in the county. There was just one vehicle involved in the incident – a blue truck owned by the Good Wood Company. It had struck something on the road on its way into town, bringing the vehicle to a sudden and violent stop, but there was no sign of what had been in its path. The windshield on the driver's side was broken and splashed with blood. It was also covered in pine needles and twigs like at Arn Bunderson's place. It had to be a coincidence, but I thought it was odd. What had caused the crash? Another vehicle?

The paramedics had already opened the door to check on the driver, so I peered inside. A big man with a salt-and-pepper beard was slumped at the wheel like he was unconscious, but he was *very* dead. From my position, I could see a big round hole in his back. There was a matching hole in the seat behind him, dripping with viscera. A shotgun at close range could do that sort of damage, but the hole was as big in his front, which was not typical of a shotgun blast. Blood was slowly dripping out of his chest cavity, where wet loops of his intestines had pooled at his feet.

Something big and sharp had pierced his body through the windshield, but whatever had done it had been removed, leaving a gory mess.

I called Dispatch to bring the coroner and some more deputies.

I waited until Melissa arrived and examined the inside of the truck before speaking to her. "That hole looks like a tree branch speared through him, but there's no damn fallen tree around here."

"Yes, it does look like this vehicle hit a tree. But trees don't leave the scene of an accident, do they?" She gave me a withering look. "Look. Here's something you missed because of the gore."

She shone a powerful flashlight onto the dead body's legs, illuminating some blood. "There's a savage cut on his upper thigh down to the bone. I can tell it happened before the accident because he tied a tourniquet with duct tape. Such injuries are something I've seen many times as a doctor. It was caused by a chainsaw."

"Ouch. You think Tom got his leg cut, then tried to drive himself to the hospital?"

"I can't know Tom's thoughts, Sheriff. I'm not psychic. However, it makes logical sense."

"Hell. If he got attacked at the sawmill, it might mean that's the primary crime scene. I'd better check it out immediately."

"I'll come with you," Melissa said.

"Don't you want to stay here?"

"Tom's dead. I'll autopsy him later. But if there are any other injured people at the sawmill, you'll need my medical skills. I'll follow your car."

I was soon driving my patrol car up the road to the sawmill. Melissa's black SUV was on my tail when I saw a sign for the Good Wood Company. I turned off onto a gravel road recently cleared of snow. The sawmill was ahead, with a huge warehouse on the left filled with raw timber. Another warehouse was on the right. I parked next to a dozen pickups owned by the employees, looking for signs of anyone around. The place looked deserted, but I could hear the screeching of the saws. The air smelled of sawdust.

Melissa parked and joined me, looking nervously in all directions. "Annie, where is everyone?"

"Don't know. Stick with me. We'll take a look around."

A blood trail led from the empty space where Tom Chandler's truck had been parked towards the sawmill. I walked that way. "Hey! Anyone here? It's Sheriff Dearborn. Can you hear me?"

I doubted anyone could hear me over the noise.

I reached the entrance to the sawmill. A moving conveyor belt was in front of me, attached to a whining circular saw. It was normally used to cut logs into sections, but it had been put to a different use that day. Instead of cutting logs into neat piles of wood, it had turned several human beings into a sticky red mound of chopped limbs, torsos, and heads. I felt the cronuts and coffee churn inside me, gritting my teeth so I didn't puke.

Behind me, Melissa moaned and vomited.

Drawing my gun, I stepped into the warehouse, looking left and right into the shadows. There were stacks of timber all over the place, as well as loud machinery. The killer could be hiding anywhere. I needed to shut down the equipment so I could hear properly. There was a red EMERGENCY STOP button on a wall. I hit it. The power cut off instantly. The circular saw jolted to a stop and the screeching ended, but another sound replaced it, the distinctive whir of a chainsaw. I turned towards the sound, raising my gun.

A skinny, blood-soaked man jumped out from behind a crate, running out of the warehouse in Melissa's direction, who was hunched over, recovering from her nausea. He was swinging a chainsaw like he wanted to decapitate her. He looked totally insane. Melissa's eyes widened in fear.

"Stop now!" I yelled, but he was yelling too.

Melissa screamed. In a second he would get to her. I couldn't let him kill her – even if she had married my ex. How could I stop the man? I thought about shooting him in the head, but it was a risky shot. If I missed, he would get to her. I could shoot him in the back, but that had no guarantee of working. No. I knew what I had to do. I aimed at his left knee and squeezed off three rounds. I prayed it would work. My shots found my target. He stumbled and fell on his own chainsaw, which wasn't part of my plan.

A moment later, the man started screaming as the blade chewed into his chest. Damn. I couldn't let him die. He had to go on trial for killing everyone. And I needed to know why he'd done it.

Unfortunately, I was too far away to do anything to save him, but Melissa did something amazing, considering he had just tried to kill her. She grabbed him by the shoulders and rolled him over, preventing the chainsaw from gutting him.

I was worried he would attack her, but he was in no fit state. His chest was cut in a dozen places, and his attention was on the chainsaw slicing into his flesh. He started convulsing as blood sprayed in a fine mist. The idiot still had his hand on the trigger, keeping it whirring and doing damage.

I ran over and yanked the chainsaw out of his hands and hurled it to a safe distance, where it stuttered and stopped. The man groaned and passed out from his wounds.

"Thanks for saving me," Melissa said. "I owe you."

"Okay. Can you keep him alive until we get him to a hospital?"

"I'll try, but we'll have to hurry."

Taking no chances, I cuffed the man before moving him into the back of my vehicle, where Melissa kept him alive until we reached the hospital. Before the medical staff rushed him away for treatment, I found his ID in the back pocket of his jeans. His name was Ken O'Leary. I didn't know him. I ran a check at the station. O'Leary had been an employee at the sawmill for six months. He had no history of violence or mental illness. Nothing about what he'd done made sense, but at least his killing spree was over. I sighed. All the families of the victims would have to be informed after they'd been fully identified. The Good Wood Company had twenty-two employees. The mound of body parts would have to be sorted out. I'd need more resources for that. I spent a few hours making phone calls.

That evening I was alone in my house, wearing the old sweats I wore for yoga, when I got a call from Deputy Rodriguez. "Uh, ma'am, I got bad news."

"The suspect died?"

"No. He's alive but unconscious. I'm afraid it's something else. I talked to some guys about him. I found out O'Leary has a solid alibi for the Bunderson murder."

"What? That's impossible. He must have done it, too."

"Sorry, ma'am. He was in the Rockaway Diner having an early breakfast when Bunderson was killed. There are a dozen witnesses and security videos. O'Leary definitely didn't kill Bunderson."

The bad news gave me an instant headache. "Okay. We'll work on it tomorrow, Sam."

"Yes, ma'am."

"You did a good job," I told him. "But *never* ever call me 'ma'am' again. I'm not your grandmother, Sam."

"Yes … Sheriff."

I hung up and stared at the TV for a while, watching the news until my eyes closed. I fell asleep on the couch, thinking about the horrors at the sawmill.

I woke in the dark, hearing a soft rustling. The TV had switched itself off, but I could see by the tiny red, green and blue lights on my Christmas tree. The rustling seemed to come from a corner of the room, where I'd placed the tree and Hanna's presents. I heard the noise again. Some of the upper branches were swaying gently like they'd caught a breeze.

For a second I wondered if a chipmunk was in the tree, but that made no sense because I'd checked it was clean before bringing it indoors. The ornaments were tinkling as the branches started bending. The whole tree rocked back and forth on its base. It was going to fall over, landing on me. I rolled off the couch a second before the tree thumped down where I'd been. Branches whipped my face, drawing blood from my cheeks. The tree thrashed like a wild animal, the trunk whipping around to knock me across the room. Next, I saw its longest branches twist to form limbs supporting its weight. Eight of them acted like legs as the tree pulled itself across my living room like a giant spider.

It had to be a dream – a nightmare – but everything was so real I couldn't take the chance. I had to get away from the Christmas tree tearing up my furniture with its claw-like branches. My phone was charging on a stand, but the tree creature was in my way. It reared up and dragged itself towards me as I scrambled to my feet and ran for the doorway into my kitchen. I heard the Christmas tree's fairy lights pop and shatter as the power cord tore out of the wall socket, plunging me into total darkness. A branch hit my legs, suddenly knocking me off feet. I slammed into an unseen chair, hurting my knees. I grabbed the chair and hurled it as a distraction, then I felt for the wall. Yes – I found the doorway and pulled myself through it. Pine needles struck my back like darts just before I escaped. My kitchen was lit by yellow light from the street. My other phone was on the counter. I grabbed it and raced for the back door, hearing the rustle-rustle of the thing squeezing its way through the doorway behind me. When I pulled open the door, I looked back long enough to see the murderous tree crawling over the floor, its branches forming gnarled claws to grab several knives from a rack. At least ten of its claws brandished weapons. It wanted to use them on me. I laughed at the absurdity, but I knew it was not a dream. That frightened me. My Christmas tree was really trying to kill me. I slammed the door closed, gasping.

Outside, I shut the door and heard it lock, hoping it

would stop the thing chasing me – or at least slow it down.

My house was on one end of the town, surrounded by quaint family homes. They were all lit up with fairy lights. Everything looked pretty and perfect, like in a Christmas movie where everyone was happy and nice to each other, but I could see and hear my house was not the only one with something dangerous inside. Whatever had transformed my tree into a killing machine had affected elsewhere. Someone was screaming in the house opposite mine and others down the street. Bill and Rose Fanner lived opposite. Before I could do anything, Bob's terrified face appeared at his bedroom window. He was trying to pull it open to get outside onto the sloped garage roof. Something green flashed behind him. Bob's neck suddenly sprayed blood on the window. The jagged tip of a branch poked through a gaping wound. More screams followed inside the house from Rose. They stopped abruptly a second later.

What the hell was happening? The world had gone mad. My next-door neighbour Zoe rushed out of her house with no clothes on, crying hysterically. She saw me and rushed over. "Annie! Help me! My Christmas tree's come alive. It killed my girlfriend!"

I could hear my own tree smashing into my door. "Zoe, it's not safe here. We have to get to the police station. Then I'll figure out what to do, I swear." I removed my sweatshirt and gave it to her. It was just long enough to cover her nakedness. The cold stung my bare arms. I was lucky I was wearing a T-shirt. The night was freezing cold. "Come on. We need to hurry."

Melissa and Shane had a house on the far side of Main Street – about a half-mile from my house. I'd never been happier to know Hanna was sleeping at their house that night – but I had to make sure she was safe. They had a Christmas tree, too. My ex had bought an even bigger than mine. As Zoe and I headed for

Main Street, I switched on my phone and called Hanna's number. I prayed she would answer it instead of letting it switch to voice mail.

"Mom?" she slurred, sounding like I'd woken her. "What's wrong?"

"This is gonna sound crazy, but you must believe me. Something evil has taken control of the Christmas trees bought from Arn Bunderson. Mine tried to kill me and I'm worried yours will try the same."

"Jeez, Mom. What drugs are you on? Have you been smoking something from the evidence room?"

"No, Hanna, I'm deadly serious. Wake your dad and Melissa. Tell them to bring you to the police station now."

"Mom, they won't believe me. You sound crazy."

"Listen to me, Hanna. You all need to keep away from the Christmas tree and get the hell out of the house. It's a matter of life or death."

"Oh, Mom, this is stupid. I'm not waking them up. Dad would be so mad. I think you should-" She paused. "Mom, I can hear *something* downstairs. You're not joking, are you?"

"No – I'm not. *Please* do what I said, Hanna."

"I'll do it, Mom."

"Text me when you're safe. I need to use my phone to warn others. I love you. Bye."

All my deputies were in my WhatsApp group. I sent them an urgent message telling them to contact me at the station. Zoe and I reached Main Street. The road out of the town was blocked by an immense pile of logs. There was something beyond it, shifting in the darkness, huge and powerful. It felt as though it saw me down to my soul. Zoe was staring at it, too.

"What is that?"

I didn't know, but I didn't want to get too close.

"The station," I reminded Zoe. "It's the safest place."

It was hot and stuffy inside the station, but I welcomed it after the cold. Darla Jones – the night dispatcher – was frantically busy behind the front desk answering calls, but she looked relieved when I hurried in with Zoe. I was momentarily spooked by the small Christmas tree at the coffee machine – until I realised it was artificial. "Darla, we've got an emergency."

"I know! Sheriff, the phones are ringing off the hook. People are reporting the weirdest things. They're saying trees are attacking them."

"They are," I said. "It's happened to me. You need to alert everyone, including the State police, the Feds and even the Forest Rangers. We need to protect and warn as many citizens as we can before we're all slaughtered." I turned to Zoe. "Could you help Darla?"

Zoe nodded. I rushed into my office, changed into my spare uniform, then came back. "Dayla, close the shutters. We need to make this place like Fort Knox. I'm gonna check outside."

I knew my guns would be useless, so I grabbed a fire axe off the wall. Then I stepped back out into the street. All around, I could hear gunshots, shouting and screaming. It was chaotic. I heard a vehicle coming and saw it was Melissa's speeding SUV. It screeched to a halt outside the station. Hanna jumped out and ran to me. "Mom!"

I hugged her as Shane and Melissa joined us. My ex-husband had a bleeding cut over his eye. Though our divorce had been acrimonious, I'd never been happier to see him. I ushered everyone into the station. Other survivors were running down the street. I was glad to see Sam Rodriguez was among them. I beckoned them inside. Up and down the street, the trees were chasing people and slaughtering any they caught. Most of the trees were decorated with fairy lights and ornaments, but some bigger ones must have come out of the forest. Some towered over the houses. I watched one sweep a huge branch through a window and spear someone inside their home. The tree pulled its screaming victim out and dropped the body onto hard asphalt, then shuffled to the next house on the block. Some people were shooting at them, but that just seemed to draw the trees' attention.

I hurried back into the station, asking some volunteers to come with me to the hardware store. We raced across the street, broke in and collected as many power tools and axes as we could carry. By then hulking trees surrounded Main Street from the forest tearing apart my little town. We had some chainsaws and useful gardening equipment, which we took back to the station and distributed to the scared citizens.

"Listen up, everyone," I said. "We've got steel shutters and reinforced concrete walls keeping them out. We've just to stay here and survive long enough to be rescued."

"Ain't nobody rescuing us," one man said. "Look. It's not just here. It's everywhere."

He held up his phone, streaming a video from a news channel. It wasn't just our town being attacked. There were reports of it happening all across America. A boy with an iPad showed everyone it was happening in other countries, too.

"We have to hope we can survive," I said. "We need some barricades for the doors and windows."

My deputies and most of the citizens helped by pushing chairs and tables into place. The building had been designed to withstand a riot, but could it prevent a tree attack?

The barricade made it impossible to look outside, but it was important to know what was there. Luckily, there were several security external cameras on all sides of the station, providing multiple views of the street from various angles. To the north, near the gas station, a gang of men were throwing gasoline bombs at some attacking trees. They successfully ignited the branches and did some damage, destroying a couple of trees, but it didn't stop the remaining trees from attacking the men, even with their branches on fire. The trees used their burning branches as weapons against the gang, setting the men on fire. They died screaming. Simultaneously, spilt gasoline ignited a pump and blew up the whole gas station, sending a fireball up into the sky, blasting out windows and rocking the ground under my feet.

After that, the large trees blocked the street and the smaller ones hunted the humans hiding in the houses. The cameras worked in low light, revealing a monstrous shape rising from the forest, watching the death and destruction. It was the thing I'd seen earlier. Something made from the forest itself.

"What's that?" I wondered aloud.

Hanna was next to me and heard my words. "Mum, I think it's a dryad."

"What's a dryad?"

"I read about them in a fantasy novel. It's the spirit of the forest. I think it's controlling all the other trees, making them hurt us. It must want revenge for all of the bad things we've done to the planet."

Slowly, the trees pushed a massive machine into the middle of the street. Once it was outside the station, a tree struck the ON button. The machine hummed. More trees dragged the surviving humans towards the machine. I watched in horror as I realised it was a wood chipper. A larger tree picked up the townspeople one by one and fed them into the spinning blades. The air filled with red mist. The slaughter went on for hours.

Hundreds died.

I feared the trees would attack us next, but nothing happened. Dawn came and the trees stopped moving, leaving the streets silent.

The dryad had gone, but its message was easy to understand.

It showed mercy and spared us, giving the human race a last chance at redemption for all we had done wrong.

THE RIPPER LEGACY

"God!" Emily said. "Is that clock accurate?"

"Yeah," Nick answered breathlessly, running his hands over her naked thighs. "Why?"

"I'm sorry." Emily reluctantly pulled away from him, rushing to the short skirt and lacy underwear she had stripped off and dropped on the carpet of Nick's office. She started dressing quickly. "My husband's doing a Ripper lecture tonight. I can't miss it."

Nick groaned. "Just another ten minutes, Ems. He won't care if you're not there. Come back over here, you naughty girl."

"I can't," she said. "I promised I'd be there."

Nick strode over to her and kissed her neck, his hand caressing her hips, tugging at her skirt, easing it down her legs. He whispered in her ear. "But I want you *now*."

Emily was very tempted to stay – but she was already half-dressed and feeling guilty for having an affair with her boss. It was such a cliché. "No. I can't." She gently slapped his hands away from her skirt. "I have to go. We have this weekend thing planned."

Nick stepped back. He looked annoyed.

"Go then," he said.

She hurried out of his office to the lift, where she adjusted her skirt and buttoned her blouse up to her neck as the lift descended to the underground parking level. Emily drove out of the exit and travelled out of London to the Wetherley Hotel. The hotel was a country manor that had been modernised into a three-star hotel by its owners. She collected her room key from the reception, dumped her bags in her room, then went searching for the conference room. It was easy to find because a life-sized Jack the Ripper figure stood beside the doors. The cardboard cut-out character was wearing a top hat and black cape – with a knife in one hand and a Gladstone bag in the other. It was creepily realistic. The Ripper's malevolent dark eyes stared at her like he wanted her to be his next victim. Her husband normally kept it at home in the garage, where it scared her every time she saw it. She felt like punching it as she walked by.

Aaron's stupid lecture had started at eight – but it was half-past eight when she sneaked into the conference room.

Emily discovered only a dozen other members of the Ripper society had bothered to show up for Aaron's lecture. They included just one new member, a shabbily dressed bearded man wearing a black anorak. There had been over three hundred active members of the society at the beginning, when Aaron created the society while a student at Oxford, but most had dropped out after a few years, leaving only the hardcore Ripperologists by the society's tenth year.

That evening her husband wore his best suit and tie, standing behind a lectern with a map of London circa 1888 projected behind him on a large screen. Emily hoped Aaron would not be upset by her late arrival when she sat next to Kyra, the only other young woman in the group, but Aaron cast his disapproving eyes over her before continuing a heated argument with a heavily tattooed member called Gary, who wore a black leather jacket and aviator sunglasses indoors. Gary was a writer of Ripper horror stories. Unlike her husband, Gary didn't attend their meetings because he wanted to solve the murders. He came to get new ideas for his short stories and novels.

Emily mouthed 'sorry' to her husband as she took off her jacket and made herself comfortable – but Aaron didn't see her apologising. He was shaking his head at something Gary had said.

Emily whispered to Kyra. "What are they arguing about?"

"Gary mentioned Lewis Carroll."

Aaron was a serious Ripperologist. He would not have liked that. He was glaring at Gary. "You are so wrong, it isn't even funny. Lewis Carroll was a *joke* suspect. He wasn't even in London when some murders happened. A much more credible suspect is Charles Allen Cross, the subject of my lecture tonight."

Gary rolled his eyes. "Oh, come on! You don't seriously think he did it, do you? He's a boring nobody!"

"He's not a boring nobody. He's a credible suspect. Can I continue, or do you want to interrupt some more?"

Gary shrugged. "Whatever."

Aaron looked around at the other members of the Ripper society, his focus stopping on Emily. She remembered his intensity and passion quickening her heart, but she did not feel that way any longer. All she saw was his obsession with the Ripper ruining their relationship. For ten years it had been all he had been interested in after leaving university. He wrote books on the Ripper, ran a website and internet forum, organised monthly Ripper society meetings, and blogged about it every day. Aaron spent more time researching the Ripper than he did with her. She was not in love with him any longer – but he had not even noticed. At least Nick noticed her.

Emily watched her husband turn to point at the screen

while pressing a key on his laptop. A section of the map enlarged to show Whitechapel in 1888. "Like I was saying before Gary *rudely* interrupted, Charles Allen Cross was here on Buck's Row, actually standing over the body of the second Ripper victim, when he was seen by another man. That witness – Robert Paul – would have definitely described Cross to the police as a suspect if Cross had not claimed to have just found the body. Cross said he had just got there and seen nobody else around – but the body was still warm ... so how did he not see or hear the killer leaving? There is only one simple explanation. Cross was Jack the Ripper."

"That's *too* simple," Gary said. "In my opinion Cross was just what he claimed to be – an innocent witness. What does everyone else think?"

More people agreed with Gary than Aaron, clearly annoying Aaron, who had expected his argument to win greater support. Emily felt sorry for her husband. She had known he had spent weeks working on that night's lecture.

"Please consider the evidence!" Aaron said. "Occam's Razor states the simplest solution is -"

"Dead boring!" another member interrupted. That was a platinum blonde woman in her mid-forties called Glenda. Glenda wore sexy clothes like Marilyn Monroe, showing off her large fake breasts – but she had a greater resemblance to the murderous Myra Hindley. "We don't want Jack to be some boring ordinary man. That's not interesting. I want it to be a conspiracy involving the Royal Family and the government. That's *exciting!*"

"What I'm saying might not be exciting," Aaron said. "But I'm after the truth."

"The truth?" Gary said, doing an obvious Jack Nicholson impression from *A Few Good Men*. "You can't handle the truth!"

His comment received laughs from some and disdained

looks from others. Not even remotely amused, Aaron slammed his fist on the lectern. "Listen to me! The evidence against Cross is strong. He lied to the police. He knew the area well because he worked nearby. His job as a cart driver made him practically invisible. He wore an apron and delivered meat for a slaughterhouse – so nobody would even think twice about seeing him with blood on his clothes. He could have done it, people! I've done a computer simulation of each murder that -"

Gary stood up and yawned. "I'm tired of this subject. We're all here to have a good weekend, right? Are we going to the bar or what, guys?"

Glenda jumped up, her breasts jiggling. "The bar!"

More people stood up.

That ended Aaron's lecture early as several people followed Gary towards the doors. Kyra stayed behind with Emily – but only until the room was almost empty. "Well, I might as well join them. Emily, you coming?"

"I'll be along soon," she said.

The lecture abandoned, nobody had a reason to stay. Everyone remaining headed to the bar, leaving Emily alone with her furious husband. She walked over to Aaron as he closed his laptop and put away his research material in a black briefcase. He was muttering something as she gently put her hands on his shoulders and rubbed his tight, tense muscles. "Don't get so upset about Gary. He's an idiot."

"But I'm right about Cross," he said. "He is a good suspect. Gary should admit I'm right. I hate that man. He doesn't come to talk seriously about the Ripper. He just comes to socialise and mock my attempts at being a professional investigator of the facts."

"Forget him," Emily said. "I was interested in what you said. Now let's go and join the others for a drink, okay?"

Aaron sighed. "Fine. Just don't expect me to be nice to Gary. He can go to hell." He slammed his briefcase shut. "By the way, why were you so late? Everything would have been a lot better if you'd been there on time. Was it your boss again, keeping you late at the office?"

"I left work at seven – but there was a traffic jam," she said, the lie flowing smoothly from her lips, while she rubbed her wedding ring. "Being late wasn't my fault. There was an accident or something. Now forget about what Gary said so we can have a good weekend."

In the hotel bar, Emily and Aaron joined a group at a table where everyone was discussing the 'Dear Boss' letters. Those letters had been the first ones to give the Whitechapel Murderer the catchier nickname Jack the Ripper. Some people thought they were a hoax written by a journalist to reignite interest in the story – but the identity of the writer had never been discovered, deepening the mystery. The newbie in the black anorak had a lot of questions.

"Where's Gary?" Aaron mumbled to Emily.

"Uh - way over there."

Wisely, Gary was sitting at another table far away, drinking beers and flirting with Glenda. It looked as though the members had split into two groups according to how they had reacted to Gary's suggestion. The pro-Gary faction were laughing and having a good time – making Emily a little jealous because they were enjoying themselves. They were clearly not talking scholarly about Jack the Ripper, like the pro-Aaron group.

There had been a time when Emily had been just as obsessed with the Ripper as Aaron. Aged thirteen, she had done some homework for her social studies class, which involved drawing a family tree. Using a genealogy website, she had discovered she was related to the Ripper's fifth victim, Mary Jane

Kelly. That fact had led to a keen interest in all things Ripper-related. At university she had joined Aaron's Ripper Society because she wanted to learn more. Aaron had been fascinated by her link to the Ripper, treating her like a celebrity. She had loved his attention. Emily remembered spending long nights with him in the university library, researching Victorian London. After a long study session, they used to sneak into the stacks to kiss and make love. Now she could hardly remember the last time her husband had shown any sexual interest in her. Right then he was showing more interest in answering the newbie's questions.

"I'm a little confused," the newbie was saying. "What exactly are the canonical murders I've heard people mentioning?"

"Most experts believe just five murders can be attributed to Jack the Ripper because they match his MO of strangling, throat-cutting and dismembering his victims. They were Polly Nichols, Anne Chapman, Elizabeth Stride, Catherine Eddowes and Mary Jane Kelly. They are the so-called canonical murders. They were several more murders in Whitechapel that could be Ripper kills – but they don't match the same MO. Martha Tabram, for example, was stabbed multiple times – but she wasn't strangled first. There was also Rose Mylett and Lizzie Davies. They ..."

Emily soon became bored by the conversation at her table because she had heard it all before. She stopped listening, choosing instead to focus on getting drunk with Kyra, who had been her best friend since they shared a room at Oxford. Kyra had joined the Ripper Society to support Emily – but over the years Kyra had developed an expert's knowledge in the subject. Kyra was a freelance journalist and Ripperologist, but she didn't talk about the Ripper endlessly. She only talked about that subject if asked. Emily appreciated that. They moved away to another table so they could chat about what they'd been doing since they last met in person.

"I haven't done much," Emily said. She nearly added: "Apart from having an affair." But she didn't say it. "You still seeing that guy – the TV presenter?"

"No," Kyra said. "He went back to his wife."

"I'm sorry."

"Don't be. He was a jerk. He never intended to leave her. He was a liar." Kyra emptied her glass of wine. "God, I wish I could find a good man. I'm sick of dating losers. You are so lucky, Emily."

"I am?"

"Absolutely. You're married to a man you love."

Emily sighed. "Lucky me."

Kyra frowned. "Hey – you look sad. What's up?"

"Our sex life is non-existent."

"Oh. But you two used to be all over each other."

"I know," Emily said. "These days we hardly do *anything* together. I'm always working and he's always researching. Hell – Kyra - you probably spend more time with him than I do because you share his interest in the Ripper. Frankly, I'm sick of hearing about the Ripper. He's like a third person in our marriage."

"Are you crying?"

"A little," she admitted, wiping her tears away before anyone else noticed. "God, Kyra, I've done something bad."

"What?"

The next words out of her mouth would have never escaped if she had not been drinking so much wine. "I've been having an affair."

Kyra looked stunned. "Wow." She lowered her voice. "How long?"

"Four months."

"With whom?"

"This guy at the office. Nick. My boss. He's married too. We just started flirting one day and then it just sort of happened."

"Does Aaron know?"

"Of course not. You're not going to say something, are you?"

Kyra shook her head. "I'd never do that. God. What are you going to do?"

"I don't know. Maybe a divorce?" She felt a sob in her throat that she had to suppress. "I don't like thinking about it. I need another drink. I'm not yet drunk enough to enjoy myself. I need another glass of wine immediately."

"I'll get it," Kyra said.

Emily stayed in the bar until midnight. The bar stayed open for another couple of hours – but she was embarrassingly slurring her words and did not want to stay up that late. She said goodnight to Kyra before approaching the table where her husband was still talking to the bearded newbie in the black anorak. "I'm going to bed, Aaron. Are you coming with me?"

"Uh – no. Just want to discuss something a bit longer."

Emily didn't bother kissing him. What would be the point? She staggered towards the lift in the reception area, where she saw Glenda waiting alone with a bottle of champagne. The door to the first lift opened after about a minute of awkward silence. They entered it together. Glenda pressed for the fourth floor. "Which floor are you on?"

"Uh – four."

"That's me, too. I guess we're all on the same floor because we booked at the same time."

"Guess so."

That was the end of their conversation. The lift opened onto a long red-carpeted corridor that had doors to the left and right. Emily's room was number 404 – which was to the left. Glenda exited and turned right. "Good night, Emily."

"'night."

Emily reached her room and struggled to find the key in her handbag. It took her a long time to locate, even though it had a plastic fob attached. She fumbled the key into the lock and opened her door, pausing to look into the darkness inside the suite. It had twin beds instead of a double because her husband liked to sleep on his own.

A giggle down the corridor made her turn her head to see Glenda disappearing into a room. "Got the champers," Glenda said before the door closed. Emily was envious. Glenda wasn't going to sleep alone. Emily stumbled over to her bed and slumped down on it, lonely and angry, seriously thinking of sexting Nick – but Nick would be at home with his wife and kids. Calling him now would be a very dumb move. Feeling very sorry for herself, Emily stripped off her clothes and crawled into her single bed, sobbing into her pillows until she slipped into unconsciousness.

"Emily ... Emily ..."

"What?"

"Time to wake up."

"Urgh. What's the time?"

"Six-thirty."

"Six-thirty?" She opened her eyes and saw her husband was already shaved and dressed. "I was sleeping. Why the hell did you wake me?"

"Breakfast's between seven and eight-thirty. It's best to be down before everyone else."

"Why?"

"It's buffet style. All the bacon and eggs will be freshly cooked if we get there early."

"Please don't talk about food. I feel sick."

"Hangover?"

"Yes. From hell."

"*From Hell*! That's the title of a Ripper film starring Johnny Depp!"

Emily could not believe he had brought up the Ripper before she had got out of bed or even woken up properly. A new record. "Go down on your own. Let me sleep a little longer."

"Come on. I gave you half an hour to get ready. I'll turn on the shower and make some tea."

She tried going back to sleep – but the sound of the shower running made it hard. Hearing the kettle boiling made it impossible. Confronted by a hot cup of tea that smelled vilely of clotted UHT milk, her stomach flipped and she rushed to the toilet just in time.

Aaron came to the doorway. "You okay, hon?"

"No – but you got me awake. Happy now?"

"You sound mad with me – but being awake is better than sleeping through a breakfast we've already paid for."

"Not to me, it isn't." Her stomach couldn't cope with a big breakfast. But she was fully awake now. By seven, she was ready to leave their suite for a very light breakfast – maybe some dry toast and fruit – so she followed Aaron into the corridor. They walked to the lift in silence. Aaron pressed the button. She pressed it too once, twice, three times.

"That won't speed it up," he said.

"Oh, shut up."

"What did I do?"

She sighed. "Let's just get down for breakfast. I'm not in the mood for talking to you this early in the morning."

The lift was coming up to their floor. Upon arriving, the door opened slowly, revealing a dark figure inside - with a knife.

It was Jack the Ripper.

"Jesus!" Emily cried out. It took her a second to realise it was the cardboard cut-out. "What the hell, Aaron? That's not funny! You scared me."

"I didn't put it there," he said. "I bet it was Gary. I should have a stern word with him."

"Forget him," Emily said. "Let's just go down now."

They squeezed into the lift with Jack the Ripper between them. Emily pressed G for the ground floor. The lift descended silently, almost like it was not moving. After a minute it reached the ground floor. Emily stepped out into the deserted reception while her husband lifted up his cardboard Ripper and carried it out. He stood holding it outside the closed and locked doors of the dining room.

Emily glared at him.

"What?" he said innocently.

"You are not bringing that thing with us for breakfast. The staff will think you are a nutter."

"Okay. I'll put Jack back outside the conference room," he said, leaving her standing alone.

She waited impatiently until Aaron returned. They stood waiting for another ten minutes. Emily paced. "This is ridiculous. We obviously came down too early."

"Not according to my watch. They should have opened up by now. Where is everyone?"

"Are you sure you have the time right?"

"Yes," he said. He walked over to the reception desk. "I'll get someone."

He rang the bell for service – but nobody appeared. Emily was bored of standing around waiting for a breakfast she didn't even want. "I'm going back to our room."

"I'll stay here."

"Whatever. You can get me when they eventually open the dining room." She stomped off towards the lift.

The fourth floor was deathly quiet when she walked back to her room. On the way, she noticed several doors were ajar, which seemed strange because nobody had come down for breakfast. Maybe there were no guests in those rooms? She stopped at Kyra's room. Her door was ajar too – so she knocked and called her name.

There was no reply – but her knock pushed the door inwards, revealing darkness. The curtains were closed. "Kyra?" Emily identified the shapes of the TV, wardrobe and bed. The bed was occupied and, for a moment, Emily believed her friend was sleeping – but something was wrong. As her eyes adjusted to the gloom, a tightness gripped her chest so she could not even scream.

Someone had sliced Kyra's neck open to the bone. One of Kyra's internal organs – a kidney or her liver – had been draped on her shoulder. More organs had been removed and left in a heap on her butchered abdomen.

Emily stared at her in shock and disbelief. Her best friend was lying in a pool of dark blood, very, very dead.

Emily staggered backwards into the corridor, trying to shout for help, but she felt as though her own throat had been cut because she could make no sounds. She gasped for breath – looking up and down the empty corridor, afraid the killer would suddenly appear. A thought hit her like a powerful blow. Call the police! Her phone was in her bag. Her bag was in her room. She had the key on her – but she was terrified of unlocking the door in case the killer was in there, waiting for her.

A noise made her look towards the lift. There was a light on. The lift was coming up. Who was inside? Was it Aaron? She hoped it was – but what if it was the killer?

She ran up to a door that was slightly open and slipped into another dark bedroom. There was a male dead body on the bed with its throat cut – but she didn't scream because she was more frightened by the unknown person coming up in the lift. Any noise would give away her hiding place. She closed the door the way she had found it and listened as the lift stopped. She thought of hiding in the room somewhere – but what if her movements made a noise? No – she was frozen behind the door. Listening as someone stepped out of the lift. The soft carpet made their footfalls almost silent. Was it the killer? She peered through the gap as the person walked in her direction. A shadow passed.

She saw it was Aaron. Relief poured through her in a warm wave as she opened the door, making her husband jump when she whispered his name. He turned around, frowning. "Nobody showed up at the reception. What are you doing in Henry's room?"

"Hiding," she said. "Aaron, someone's killing everyone."

"What?"

"Look."

She stepped aside so he could see beyond her into the room. Aaron studied the crime scene like he was used to seeing dead bodies in hotel rooms. "My God! His wounds are like the Ripper's first victim."

"Kyra's dead too," she said. "I think someone's been in every room, leaving the doors ajar after killing the people inside. W-what are we going to do?"

"We'll get the police." Aaron patted his pockets. "Damn. I left my phone in our room. Do you have yours?"

"No. It's also there."

"Okay – let's get our phones and call the police."

"What if the killer is waiting in our room?"

"I don't know," he said. "You want to risk it or just get out of here?"

"Out of here," she said.

"Lift or stairs?"

"Not the lift. We'd be trapped."

"The stairs then."

"Okay," she said.

Just then she heard a door opening down the corridor. They both stared as a woman appeared wearing a hotel bathrobe, last night's clothes bundled in her hands. It was Glenda. She grinned nervously. "Oh, hi. You caught me doing the 'walk of shame'!"

"You're okay?" Emily said.

"Yeah," Glenda said. "Why wouldn't I be?"

"Everyone's dead – except you and us."

"What are you talking about?"

"They've been murdered in their sleep," Aaron said. "Their throats were cut – like Jack the Ripper's victims."

Glenda should have been shocked – but she continued walking towards them. "That's a sick joke, Aaron."

"I'm not joking." He opened the door of Kyra's suite. "Look if you don't believe me."

Finally, Glenda accepted what they were saying. "She's dead. Really dead. Have you called the police?"

"Not yet," Aaron said. "We left our phones in our room. Do you have yours?"

Glenda nodded. "Here. You report it. I can't even think of the name of the hotel. My head's spinning. I can't believe everyone's dead. I'd better tell Gary."

Aaron made the call while Glenda went back to the room to get Gary. Gary came out half-dressed, wearing only his jeans and socks. Even though he had been told everyone was dead, Gary had to have a look for himself in several rooms. "They've all been butchered. Wow. It's like the Ripper's alive again."

He almost sounded excited.

Cool and collected, Aaron reported the murders while Emily looked up and down the corridor, fearing the killer would come back. She felt safer with four of them still alive – but none of them had a weapon until Gary went back to his room and brought back a mini fire extinguisher.

Aaron ended his call. "The police are coming right now. They should be here in fifteen minutes."

Gary swore. "Fifteen minutes? We could all be dead by then. Let's get out of here *now*. Come on, Glenda. Let's go."

He hurried to the lift, with Glenda following him. Emily and Aaron warned them to come back – but they didn't listen. Gary reached the lift with Glenda right behind him. As soon as Gary pressed the button, the door opened. Gary stepped in – but Glenda was reluctant.

"What if the killer's downstairs, Gary?"

"Listen to me," Emily said. "We can't go down in the lift. It's too predictable. We have to get out another way."

Glenda nodded in agreement. "Any ideas?"

"The stairs?" Aaron suggested.

Gary stepped out of the lift. "You lead the way."

"No," Emily said. "The stairs go to the same place – the reception area. We need to think of something better. I know! The fire exit. It leads directly outside down the side of the building."

There was a sign pointing in the direction of the nearest fire exit – around a corner to their left. Emily and Aaron led the way down the corridor until the exit was in view. There was a metal bar across the exit to be pushed only in emergencies. This situation definitely constituted an emergency. Emily and Aaron pushed the bar together and opened the door, stepping out into the cold, fresh air, triggering an alarm. Emily looked down at the car park below. In the distance, she could see flashing lights on the road leading to the hotel. She hurried down the stairway, holding her husband's hand.

Just one police vehicle showed up in response to the 999 call – until the full extent of the situation was understood by the authorities. Soon after, the hotel was surrounded by police vehicles and ambulances. A paramedic checked Emily for shock at the scene. Her blood pressure was high – but not dangerously high. She wanted to go home – but a forensics officer had to examine her before letting her leave.

The massacre at the hotel was the biggest story on the news all week – but the police didn't release many details at first. The total dead was estimated at over eighty by the media, but the police would not confirm that figure until they dad done a complete investigation. A few days passed before a detective visited Emily and Aaron to give them an update. Eighty-four people had been killed. They included all the staff and most of the guests.

"It appears the killer started with the staff on duty during the night. They had their throats cut. Then the killer used the spare keys to go room to room, murdering everyone in their beds. They were all killed very quickly – so they could not wake the other guests. The survivors had one thing in common that probably saved their lives. You were not sleeping alone. We believe the killer did not risk attacking you because the other person in the room might have woken up during the attack."

"Do you have a suspect?" Aaron said.

The detective nodded. "There was one guest unaccounted for among the dead and survivors. This man."

The detective showed them a photograph of a bearded

man. "Do you recognise this man?"

"Yes," Aaron said. "He was a new member."

"We didn't find his body," the detective said. "His name is Eric Casavian. We found some things at his home address that make us believe he was the man responsible."

Emily was curious. "What sort of things?"

"I can't go into details," the detective said. "I'll just say his internet history is quite disturbingly violent. He had a collection of over 10,000 horror movies. He recently joined your society, Aaron?"

Aaron nodded. "That's right."

"What can you tell me about him?"

"Not much. We only met at the conference. We had a long conversation about Jack the Ripper on the night of the ... massacre. I explained to him what the canonical murders were. He didn't seem to think that five murders were a lot, considering how infamous the Ripper has become. He knew a lot about other serial killers like Ted Bundy. Do you think he murdered everyone just to outdo the real Ripper?"

"I don't know his motive," the detective said. "But what you've told me is helpful."

"Do you think you'll catch him?"

"We just don't know."

As one of the survivors, Emily was the focus of a great deal of media attention in the weeks that followed. At first, she was portrayed as a brave survivor – but then a tabloid exposed her affair with Nick. Twitter trolls launched a merciless attack on her – many users somehow blaming her for the massacre - but that didn't hurt as much as Aaron's reaction. He moved out of their home.

She didn't lose her job because of her affair – but she was

transferred to another department where she never saw Nick. For months she spent most of her time in her office working late because she hated going back to an empty house. She didn't know if she wanted to stay married to Aaron – but she hated the hurt she had caused him. Working hard was something to distract her from the mess she had made of her life.

She spent much time using her office computer visiting internet forums, curious to see what people were thinking about the murders. Most people thought Eric Casavian had done them to become as famous as the real Jack the Ripper. Others believed he was just a psycho. A small group believed Eric Casavian was not the killer - but another victim, as yet undiscovered. Some believed Casavian's body had been dismembered and his head taken away by the real killer to fool the police into thinking he had done it – but that theory had no grounding in the evidence. None of the body parts had DNA matching the DNA evidence collected from Eric Casavian's flat in Camden. In the darkest parts of the internet, wild theories spread like school gossip as thousands of people speculated about the identity of the murderer. One group suspected Gary because he had used the murders as publicity to sell his latest novel. Aaron had benefited from the publicity in a perverse way, too. His website had received 5000 new subscribers and his Twitter account had gained 170,000 new followers. He had also been invited to be a guest speaker at a convention of Ripperologists held in Las Vegas. He had become a celebrity. Was that a possible motive for the murders? Fame?

There was no evidence to prove it – but a leaked police report did make Emily wonder about her husband. The murder weapon used to kill everyone had been a 16-inch knife taken from the hotel's kitchen. If Eric Casavian had been the killer and he had planned the murders ahead of time, why did he not bring his own murder weapon?

The answer to that question haunted her mind.

For weeks she had been avoiding Nick - but she encountered him one evening when they had to share the lift going down to the underground car park. It was an awkwardly silent ride down. The underground parking area was dark and smelled of petrol fumes. Most employees of Waterman-Cooper had left hours ago – so just a handful of cars remained in the cavernous space. A weak strip of lights in the middle provided light – leaving most of the empty spaces in gloom. Emily hated parking underground because it reminded her of the dark streets of Whitechapel where Jack the Ripper had stalked his victims. Nick broke the silence as they walked towards their cars.

"I'm getting divorced."

"Oh. I'm sorry."

"Thanks. How are you and Aaron?"

"We're separated."

He nodded. "You want to get back with him?"

"I honestly don't know."

"What are you doing tonight?"

"I'm going to the gym. Taking self-defence lessons. I've been frightened ever since the murders happened."

"That's sensible." Nick stopped at his car. "Well, have a good night."

"You too," she said, walking on. She waved at Nick's black BMW when it drove by, heading for the exit. Then she was alone. Emily had become frightened of being alone anywhere – so she hurried towards her car. Her high heels echoed in the cavernous space, making her extremely aware of the silence all around her. She increased her speed, feeling her heart thudding as she approached her parking space in the darkest corner. She had her key ready when she slowed down to look around, checking nobody was following her. She feared Jack the Ripper would be hiding behind a concrete pillar, waiting to leap out to strangle her. She saw nobody. There was an electronic beep when her car unlocked – but she didn't get in straight away. A quick look into the back proved to her that nobody was hiding inside before she risked entering the vehicle. Once inside, she locked herself in, breathing a sigh of relief. She was safe. At least there was no Jack the Ripper in her car today.

Just then the phone in her bag vibrated – startling her - almost giving her a heart attack. She swore to herself before taking the phone out to look at the screen. One new text message from Nick.

I missed you.

Emily hesitated before texting back.

Missed you too.

They went for a drink a few days later.

One night she was alone in her office when she thought she heard a door banging down the hallway. Since the massacre, every little unexplained sound made her nervous – so she opened her door and looked down the dark hallway. It was deserted.

"Hello?" she called out. "Who's there?"

Nobody answered – but she had heard a door *bang*. Someone was there. Was it a late-night cleaner? Or was the killer coming back to kill her? She walked down the hallway armed with a letter opener. She had her smartphone in her other hand, ready to call 999 if there was anyone there – but she checked each office and found them deserted.

Probably a noise on another floor.

Probably.

There was another noise.

Ding.

The lift doors opened.

Nick was inside.

"I got your text," he said.

"What text?"

"You sent me a text asking me to come up."

"No, I didn't."

"Then -"

It was his last word.

Like in a nightmare, a black-caped figure appeared from behind a partition and stepped behind Nick, slicing his throat twice, opening his carotid artery, spraying his blood. Nick choked on his blood as he fell onto his knees. The killer stood behind Nick as he bled out. Nick struggled to close the savage wound – his eyes imploring Emily to help him.

She wanted to save Nick's life – but the Ripper would kill her if she moved forward. She had to call the police instead. She pressed 'send' - but nothing happened. She looked at the smartphone and realised it was the same model as her own smartphone – but it wasn't her phone. It was not connected to any network. It was dead. It must have been swapped when she was out of her office.

Jack the Ripper stepped around Nick's body, holding a Gladstone bag, his face hidden under a top hat, his long, sharp knife dripping blood.

Emily saw his beard and thought for a second it was Eric Casavian – until she realised it was just a disguise because the eyes behind the disguise were all too familiar.

"Glenda?"

"Hello, Emily."

"Why are you doing this?"

"Why? Jack the Ripper is the most famous serial killer of all time – for only killing five people. I've always wanted to do something like that – to leave my mark on history. Everyone is talking about me, and tonight's murders will just add to my notoriety."

"You maniac. You killed those people to become *notorious*?"

"Not just notorious – a legend. The secret of becoming a

legend is creating an unsolvable crime – a mystery that is so horrific the world remembers it long after I'm gone. I decided to create a new legend. A new Ripper. I planned every aspect for months so I could provide myself with an alibi and a mysterious missing suspect. Gary provided the perfect alibi by drinking my drugged champagne. Getting rid of Eric Casavian's body was technically much harder. I needed to get his body out of the hotel and transport him in a van to a place where nobody would find it. That was hard to do on my own – but it was worth it. So far, my plan has been a spectacular success. Tonight, your tragic death will add to my legend."

"You're insane, Glenda."

"No – I'm famous and infamous." Glenda laughed as she advanced on her. "Today's a special day, Emily. You'd know that if you cared about the Ripper as much as I do. It's the ninth of November – the anniversary of Mary Jane Kelly's death. Imagine what the police will think when they find you butchered, just like her. How tragic! They'll think Eric Casavian came back for you. You will be his final victim before he disappears forever, leaving just his DNA at the scene."

Emily turned and ran for her office.

Glenda chased her down the hall.

Emily sprinted.

The door looked so far away.

Run, run, run.

Emily made it to the door a second before Glenda, hearing behind her the swish of a knife.

Thirty seconds later, a window shattered on the fortieth floor of the Waterman-Cooper building. A woman tumbled out, battered and bruised, screaming as she plunged towards the ground.

She was wearing a black cape and flapped her arms like a bat – but it didn't help her fly.

WRITING HORROR 102

I stopped typing and stared at the screen. I'd done it. I'd written the first draft of a story in sixty minutes like the masked madman had demanded. Sweat dripped off my head as I leaned back, resting my aching fingers.

"There! I did it!"

The masked man was leaning over my shoulder, reading my words, catching up with the last few sentences.

I dreaded what he would think – but I had to ask him his opinion. "What do you think? Do you like it?"

The masked man sighed. "It has a beginning, a middle and an end – but not necessarily in the right order. It's rough – but I'm satisfied. I won't have to kill you. Not this time."

"Not this time? What does that mean?"

"It means you did well today – but I'll come back again tomorrow if you fail to write something."

The experience had been a nightmare – but now that it was over – now that I had done it – I felt elated. There was nothing more satisfying than finishing a story, the feeling of achieving something, making something from nothing. I hated the madman – but I needed to say something before he left.

"Thank you. I couldn't have done that without you."

"I know. You needed the motivation." The masked man headed for the door – but he stopped because someone was turning the knob.

"My friend's here now," he said. "Goodbye and good luck."

Another man entered my study, also wearing a mask. He was holding a long iron stick with a sharp end. Apart from the mask, he was naked. His massive, muscular body was covered with tattoos. They looked like words scrawled up and down his arms and over his chest and down his legs. They were all spelt incorrectly. *Seperately* and *accidently* were tattooed on his wrists. *Recieve* and *definitaly* were on his chest. The writer in me noticed the errors and mentally corrected them. Every tattoo was similar. They were words or phrases or complete sentences with some kind of spelling or grammar mistake. An illiterate moron must have done his tattoos.

"It's my turn now," the new man said as he moved closer to me. "All writers know me and fear me. I am the one who judges."

He stood beside me, staring at my computer's screen, pointing the stick at my finished work, then at my chest. The sharp point pressed into my chest, sending a needle of pain into me.

"This story is not ready. I'm giving you sixty minutes to make me happy. Or I will stab you with my stick in some very soft and vulnerable places until you scream for mercy. The time starts now."

"Wait, wait! I don't understand. I wrote a story like the other guy asked. What else can I possibly do?"

"What else? *What else?* You should know!"

"Know *what?*"

"You must please me," he said. "You must improve it. Make it better. Polish your manuscript until it shines."

"How?"

"Do you see my tattoos?"

"Yes, of course. They're ... very nice."

"VERY NICE? NO. They are an abomination. THEY ARE WRONG. They will show you what to avoid when you correct your manuscript to my satisfaction. Do not allow any of the errors written on my skin in your next draft. I will cause infinite pain if you fail me. DO YOU UNDERSTAND NOW?"

"Yes, yes," I said. "Just tell me one thing. Who are you?"

He grinned behind the mask, revealing rows of razor teeth.

"I am the creature every writer fears."

"Yes, but what's your name?"

"Isn't that obvious?"

"No."

"They call me *The Proofreader*."

AFTERWORD

John Moralee lives in England, where his short fiction has appeared in magazines and anthologies including *The Mammoth Book of Jack the Ripper Stories*, *Clockwork Cairo*, and the British Fantasy Society's magazine. Several collections of his stories and his novels are available as Kindle ebooks and paperbacks. They include the horror titles *The Bone Yard and Other Stories*, *Journal of the Living*, and *Bloodways*.

THANK YOU FOR BUYING THIS BOOK!

Printed in Great Britain
by Amazon